"Well," she said, **"If you brought me all this way to fire me, consider your goal achieved. If you don't mind, I'll take my leave now, *Your Royal Majesty*."**

She was proud of the amount of scholarly disdain she infused into the words.

The king remained unfazed. "In fact, and unfortunately, I did not. If it were that simple, I could have sent a note. You are here because we have been searching for you for some weeks, to no avail, only to have you stroll into the castle of your own accord."

"That's absurd. My interview was scheduled six months ago, and I am by no means in hiding." A part of her took note of the fact that she was arguing with the king, and in front of an audience no less, but that part wasn't strong enough to pull in the reins.

The king's nostrils flared. "The error has been corrected. We may move on."

"Move on with what?" Mina asked, unsure if she even wanted to know the answer.

"Our wedding."

The Queen's Guard

Romance comes to the royal palace!

When scholarly Mina Aldaba is stolen from a job interview and immediately married to the king of Cyrano, her life is totally upended. But as she adjusts to palace life, her two elite guards, Helene d'Tierrza and Jenna Moustafa, become not only her constant companions but also firm friends.

These three women will discover every inch of their strengths as they each navigate the rocky waters of romance...

Read Mina and King Zayn's story in
Stolen to Wear His Crown

And look out for Hel's and Jenna's stories

Coming soon!

Marcella Bell

———

STOLEN TO WEAR
HIS CROWN

HARLEQUIN
PRESENTS

Recycling programs
for this product may
not exist in your area.

ISBN-13: 978-1-335-89425-0

Stolen to Wear His Crown

Copyright © 2020 by Marcella Bell

This edition published by arrangement with Harlequin Books S.A.

For questions and comments about the quality of this book,
please contact us at CustomerService@Harlequin.com.

Harlequin Enterprises ULC
22 Adelaide St. West, 40th Floor
Toronto, Ontario M5H 4E3, Canada
www.Harlequin.com

Printed in U.S.A.

Marcella Bell lives in the mostly sunny wilds of southern Oregon with her husband, children, father and three mismatched mutts. The dry, hot summers and four distinct annual seasons of the region are a far cry from the weird rainy streets of Portland, OR, where she grew up, but she wouldn't trade her quirky mountain-valley home for anyplace else on the earth. As a late bloomer and a yogini, Marcella is drawn to romance that showcases love's incredible power to transform.

This is Marcella Bell's debut book for Harlequin Presents—we hope that you enjoy it!

To Eileen M. K. Bobek and the Romance Rebels.

CHAPTER ONE

Mina Aldaba smoothed her palms over her hair as she took a deep breath. The motion wouldn't do anything against the strengsth and determination of her curls to frizz—even if there was enough moisture in her palms to give it some hold—but it felt purposeful. On the other side of the ornately carved door in front of her sat the men and women of Parliament—the people whose decision would dictate whether or not she finally kept her promise to her father.

Like her hair, she was determined and untamable. She had done everything she could, with a full heart and to the very best of her ability—and that had carried her to this side of the door, inches away from the chance to achieve everything she had ever wanted.

The rest was up to the men and women inside.

The thought set off a series of stuttering palpitations in her chest—and not the kind that could ever be confused with excitement.

This next part was up to fate. The only thing she could do was be herself, trust her knowledge, and hope that that would carry her through. Unfortunately, faith wasn't one of her stronger virtues. She hadn't gotten to this side of the door by wishing. She'd done it by force of will and desire, continuous studying and practice, so she would be ready to deliver when the opportunity came.

Now was that opportunity.

She could steel her spine even if she couldn't calm her stomach.

She wore her usual black pantsuit and white blouse. Selecting one size up and choosing a square cut lent her hyper-feminine figure some much-needed gravitas. The hard lines of the design concealed any hint of curve—which she appreciated, given her very round derrière and rather Rubenesque chest. Dressing her figure for academia—or, more accurately, concealing her figure for academia—was a challenge that she hadn't anticipated when she'd decided to become a scientist at twelve years old.

Still, one had to accept what one had.

She would never forget the day a female colleague had taken her aside about it, though.

"You're going to have to do something about all of that."

Her fellow doctoral candidate had spoken blithely as she'd gestured in a vague circle toward Mina's jeans-clad rear and her breasts with a long red fingernail.

"It's just too much," she'd added. *"You'll never be taken seriously."*

At the time, the words had stung, but Mina was grateful for them. Her colleague had been right. The thin old uni sweatshirt she'd been wearing that day had stretched across her full chest, and her jeans had been form-fitted. She'd looked like the student she had always been, rather than the professional academic she was becoming, and the world she'd been about to enter was cutthroat, old-fashioned, and antagonistic—especially if you happened to have been born with female anatomy.

As soon as she had transformed her attire, her work had begun to garner more attention. Her male colleagues, it appeared, had been able to focus on it, rather than her.

Thankfully, she had mastered those ropes long ago—so well, in fact, that she was now in line to reap the highest professional reward: an interview for the appointment of an adviser to the King of Cyrano.

In preparation, her dense chocolate-brown curls had been ruthlessly brushed back from her face, heavily gelled, and confined into a thick French braid. Today—a day in which when she couldn't afford to have even a single hair out of place—she had used nearly double the amount of product to tame the springy, indomitable mass.

She had learned long ago to avoid putting her hair in a bun. Too many academics harbored sexy librarian fantasies.

The combination of the suit and the braid created a no-nonsense image—that of a serious academic. It was precisely what Mina wanted to project. Especially since she was the youngest candidate ever to sit for a parliamentary interview—and only the second woman ever nominated.

The door cracked open, and a page popped his perfectly coiffed head out.

Standing too close to the door, Mina jumped back with a quiet squeak.

The page lifted an eyebrow. "They'll be ready for you in just moment, Dr. Aldaba."

She nodded, replying, "Thank you," but the young man had already gone back inside.

Mina took another deep breath, her mind spinning. *It's almost time, Papa.*

She felt, rather than heard, the ghostly whisper of his reply: *"Cyrano is counting on you."*

Though he was long gone, her father's words were as alive as ever in her heart and mind. He'd said the same thing before every one of the significant milestones he had been alive to witness. That had amounted to thirteen years' worth of first places, gold stars, and academic honors. And then no more.

Mina shook her head, trying to clear it. There would be time for bittersweet melancholy later. Thirteen years might not have been long to have a father, but it had been long enough for them to develop a shared dream—one that she was determined to see to fruition today.

She had gone over potential interview questions for ten hours the previous day, digging up and scouring over old questionnaires from dawn until dusk, taking only short breaks for meals.

She had gone to bed at a reasonable hour, awoken early, and eaten a balanced breakfast, and then spent another hour in preparation before leaving her apartment for the interview.

The door opened again, this time fully. The page stepped into the hall and gestured for her to enter. "They are ready for you, Dr. Aldaba."

Her stomach lurched, but this time she merely nodded to the page with a confidence she didn't feel. "Thank you," she said, her voice steady and strong despite the butterflies rioting in her gut.

She walked in.

If all went well, she would walk out into a new future.

"Members of Parliament," she said, once she stood beside the interview seat. She had settled on that form of address after practicing every single acceptable salutation listed in Cyrano's official protocols. Giving the appropriate formal bow, she added, "I am honored to be here before you today."

She sat in the provided chair. It had a plain wood frame and legs, with leather cushions studded onto its seat and backrest. To its left sat a small side table, set with a microphone and a bottle of water.

Years of declining invitations and losing friendships for the sake of study flashed through her mind—as well as the exhaustion of her constant efforts to cultivate her academic image. To get here had required near-continuous drive, laser-like focus, and every ounce of passion she had. She had lived with singular tunnel vision, blocking out the rest of the world, for this moment.

And then the vetting began.

Two hours later the open question session ended, followed by a five-minute break before the voting.

Silence and time stretched on while Mina waited, stiff-backed, wrung-out, and entirely at their mercy.

Five minutes and an entire lifetime later, Parliament returned and the vote began. First, in the far upper right of the assembly, a green light flickered on. Then, in the middle of the room, another. Then, like a sea of green gently flashing to life, every light in the room turned green.

A tingling sensation filled her body, running the length of her skin and making her feel as weightless as if she were flying through thin, icy air, with the wind brushing against her skin, her mind scattered and light.

She had done it. She had just been appointed advisor to the King of Cyrano.

The prime minister stood and the rest of the people in the room rose from their seats, Mina included.

"Congratulations, Dr. Aldaba," he said. "Your appointment has been approved. We know you will be a credit to Cyrano and advise our King wisely."

There was no stopping the wide smile that broke across her face as she bowed, saying, "Thank you, Members of Parliament, it will be my honor to serve."

In her mind, she screamed, *We did it, Papa!*

And then the thick antique door came crashing inward, slamming onto the tiled floor with an earsplitting crack.

Men in riot gear rushed into the room—a wave of Kevlar and gunmetal-gray that tackled Mina to the ground before she could suck in enough air to scream.

An officer yanked her arms back, pressed a

knee into her spine, and secured zip ties around her wrists and ankles.

"What is the meaning of this?" the prime minister demanded. "You cannot barge into Parliament like this!"

One of the officers responded, "King's business, sir."

Another representative shouted, "Excuse you! This is the House of Parliament. Our business takes precedence here!"

Even so, Mina was lifted none too gently and trundled away from the nightmare that her greatest dream had become.

After a dizzying series of twisting hallways and stone passageways, she and her captors arrived at their destination. At least, she deduced it was their destination when they deposited her on the floor in front of another large wooden door, this one just as thick, but humble compared to the door of Parliament. They cut her free from the zip ties.

"You are to go inside," one of the men in riot gear said.

Mina stood, did her best to straighten herself out, and reached a shaking hand out to touch the door. When her fingers touched wood, it was as if the world turned over. Her heart tumbled with the sense that a different reality lay on the other side.

Sucking in a slight gasp of air against sudden

vertigo, she pressed her palm against the door. It slid open silently at the slight pressure of her hand, revealing an intimate room. The scent of fading incense filled her nostrils as her eyes adjusted to the dimmer light inside.

A red-carpeted center aisle with pews along either side led to a slightly raised dais in front of an ornate altar. As the image came into focus the details coalesced in Mina's mind: flickering candles, thick velvet, pews... She was in one of the castle's many chapels.

A cluster of figures stood on and below the dais, and they were all staring at her.

"Go on then," the officer said from behind her, giving her a nudge in the back.

Mina took a few halting steps into the chapel before once again squaring her shoulders.

No one spoke.

Even the administrative clip of her sensible heels was muted by the aged red carpet of the aisle.

As she neared, the cluster of people became more defined. Two men stood on the dais: the taller dressed from head to toe in midnight-black, the shorter one, older, dressed in bright white vestments. The Archbishop of Cyrano. Four others stood below the dais, arranged in front of the two men in a crescent pattern. Two men and two

women—each of them wearing the indigo uniform of the Royal Guard.

Which means the man in black is the…

Mina's gaze darted toward the man to find his
eyes already waiting for hers.

His were violet and smoldering, confirming
the descriptions she had read in magazines and
dismissed as fluff. His jaw was clean-shaven, his
caramel skin smooth enough to run her fingers
along. The thought was so un-Mina-like, it startled her from the spell of his face.

His stare was unwavering. His eyes bored into
hers. His jaw was clenched and tense, as if carved
from living granite, but she was no longer so en-
thralled that she couldn't take in the additional
details of his expression.

Faint lines of displeasure creased either side of
his mouth, and a slight line formed between his
sword-straight thick black brows as he took her
in. His eyes held heat, but there was no welcome
in their warmth.

Mina had imagined her moment of meeting
the King countless times over the years. It had
been a core component of her greatest dream for
so long that the image was virtually woven onto
the back of her eyelids.

In her imagination, she executed a perfect bow
and rose, somberly accepted as his newest advisor.

In reality, she was the worse for wear, for having been dragged before him by Cyrano's version of a SWAT team, and very much in doubt as to her welcome.

Circumstances couldn't always be ideal, however. So, gathering together the shreds of her dignity, Mina once again straightened her shoulders, steeled her spine, and then dropped into the flawless half-bow of a royal councilor to the King.

As she rose, tendrils of the King's scent swirled around her—a mesmerizing combination of leather and oak, mixed with something smooth and expensive that caught her attention even through the years of burnt incense in the chapel. It slid like silk along her senses—a flavor, a temperature, and a color all at once—and it was all she could do to remain steady as she came upright.

One look at the monarch's face, however, told her that something more than her unusual reaction to his presence was wrong. Instead of the coolly cordial distance she'd always imagined the King would exude upon their meeting, he radiated a furious intensity that almost took her aback.

He wasn't merely bothered by her. He was angry.

Holding back the frown that wanted to crease her own brow, she addressed him. "Your Grace…"

Without a smile, he replied, "It's Your Royal Majesty."

His voice was a smooth baritone that stirred something deep in her core, which was likely why it took her longer than usual to process his rejoinder.

As she did, her frown broke through her hold on it. Keeping her voice controlled, she said, "Excuse me?" She tilted her head to one side, ever so slightly.

The King looked bored. "The proper address is Your Royal Majesty. And it's customary for a woman to curtsy, rather than bow, before the King."

Her frown deepened. He was correct—the exception to the rule being female Members of Parliament and members of the King's advisory council.

For reasons she did not fully understand, rather than attempt to smooth the situation, she decided to point it out. Tersely. "Apologies, Your Royal Majesty. As a newly appointed member of your advisory council, I chose the more standard salutation."

Rather than looking chastened, as she'd expected, the King scoffed, adding casually, "You're fired. Effective immediately. You may go down in history as having had the shortest ever tenure on the advisory council."

His words, tossed out so cruelly, hit her like a bullet in the chest. She felt the telltale pressure of tears forming in the back of her eyes but refused to allow them free. Fate, it was becoming clear, would not be satisfied until it had trampled every last piece of her dreams into the dirt.

She wasn't supposed to meet the King for months, and when she finally did, it was supposed to be in the comfort of the council chambers—not a cramped chapel with the Archbishop, politely ignoring their exchange, mere steps away.

And, while she had never expected friendship—he was the King, after all—she had at least expected basic professional decorum and respect.

Instead, he had insulted her.

"Of course," he went on, after taking her in from head to toe, with a faint flare to his nostrils, "a curtsy would have been ridiculous in that suit. You deserve credit, at least, for selecting the path of least clownishness. Given your...presentation, I imagine that must be a challenge."

Mina quietly gasped, her mouth dropping open at the same time as her eyebrows drew together.

Years of effort and sacrifice flashed before her eyes—all of it gladly given for the opportunity to advise the arrogant man who now stood before her.

Her father's words echoed again in her mind: *"Cyrano is counting on you."*

If this was the King, there was little she could do for Cyrano.

It had been naive of her to imagine a paragon for a monarch. She should have known better. Vast wealth and privilege weren't known for instilling integrity and character into individuals, but for some reason she had always imagined the King would be the kind of man who listened.

She had been mistaken. But she'd encountered enough bullies throughout her career to know when it was time to stand up for yourself.

"Well," she said, "if you brought me all this way to fire me, consider your goal achieved. If you don't mind, I'll take my leave now—*Your Royal Majesty*." She was proud of the amount of scholarly disdain she infused into the words.

The King remained unfazed. "In fact—unfortunately—I did not. If it were that simple I would have sent a note. You are here because we have been searching for you for some weeks, to no avail. Only to have you stroll into the castle of your own accord."

"That's absurd. My interview was scheduled six months ago, and I am by no means in hiding."

A part of her took note of the fact that she was arguing with the King, and in front of an audience no less, but that part wasn't strong enough to pull in the reins.

The King's nostrils flared. "The error has been corrected. We may move on."

"Move on with what?" Mina asked, unsure if she even wanted to know the answer.

"Our wedding."

He broke their visual connection for the first time since he'd established it to look at his watch, and Mina felt the absence as a physical experience—though his words overwhelmed even that novel experience.

"Our wedding...?" she croaked.

The King tsked. "Reports of your intelligence seem to have been greatly exaggerated. Look around you. This chapel is certainly not where I meet with advisory council members."

Mina's mouth dropped open once again, and he observed her with a mild grimace.

"The papier-mâché box of a suit is bad enough. The fish look doesn't improve it."

Mina's mouth snapped shut, and her eyes narrowed.

"Are you nearsighted, as well? We can have that fixed...though the recovery will be long. That might be for the best, though. Give you more time to acclimate. Glasses make you look older than your age, you know."

He said all this matter-of-factly, more akin to a man examining livestock he'd just purchased than a king speaking to his...to his what?

Confusion crinkled Mina's forehead even as her eyes stung at his words. And, yes, she *did* know—though she wasn't vain or naive enough to blame it on the glasses.

At thirty-six, she wasn't young.

She had skipped being young to secure her disastrous interview before Parliament.

Closing her eyes on a sigh, Mina brought her fingers up to rub her temples. None of this made any sense.

"I think there has been some mistake," she said. "My name is Dr. Mina Aldaba. Six months ago, after applying for review, I was invited to interview for a position on your council—"

Taking a step down from the dais, one step closer to her, the King cut her off with a raised hand. "We know who you are. Dr. Amina Aldaba, only daughter of Ajit and Elke Aldaba. And, while there certainly has been a mistake, it is not ours."

His eyes chilled momentarily, and Mina realized she preferred his fire to his ice.

As if he could read her thoughts, he once again captured her gaze, his eyes warming.

She couldn't look away.

Lost in a sea of violet, she felt electric tingles ran up and down her spine, her entire body aware of the narrow distance between them.

His nostrils flared and his eyes darkened, some

new emotion wrestling for dominance with the irritation that had simmered in them from the moment they'd met.

But he merely said, "There is no mistake—and you're late. Let's get on with this."

The King turned to the Archbishop, whom Mina had all but forgotten in the intensity of their exchange.

Her cheeks heated in embarrassment at behaving like a fawning teen in front of the holy man, but the archbishop only emanated an aura of kindness and acceptance.

There, at least, things were as expected.

His voice threaded with iron, the King turned to the older man and said, "Archbishop, are you prepared to begin?"

"Begin?" Mina interjected.

The Archbishop gave Mina a look of apology, but nodded to the King. "Yes. *Your Royal Majesty.*"

Mina felt a little jolt of triumph at the censure in the holy man's tone. At least she wasn't the only one appalled by the monarch's behavior.

"I, Archbishop Samuel, solemnly consecrate the agreement entered into by King Alden of Cyrano, and Ajit Aldaba, declaring their intent that their two families be joined through the sacred bond of marriage." He turned to the King. "Zayn Darius d'Argonia, King of Cyrano…"

The King said nothing.

"Welcome Amina Elin Aldaba as your wife and Queen. Care for her, treat her as your equal consort in all ways, and your union will blossom, a blessing to all of Cyrano."

Mina broke out into a cold sweat from head to toe.

Consort? Queen? Wife?

He had said "wedding," but that was absurd. They had never even met before.

The Archbishop continued, his words swirling around in her mind, spoken in her native tongue, yet completely incomprehensible.

She was supposed to be an advisor to the King. Not his wife.

The Archbishop turned to Mina, and the room reeled. King Zayn steadied her elbow with his large, firm hand, the heat of his skin burning through the thick starched fabric of her suit jacket, his eyes on her, pinning her in place like a butterfly with the needle of his violet gaze. The pressure of his touch was gentle, though, even if his expression was mocking.

"Amina Elin Aldaba. Grace smiles upon the woman who looks to her husband as her King. May you ever look to your husband as your King, with your eyes filled with love. Honor and support him, and in turn you will honor and support Cyrano. Before God we celebrate this fruition of the promise your fathers made, joining your families, for evermore, in holy matrimony. May your union be one of love and laughter. May your marriage be blessed with children, and may your reign be long and fruitful."

Mina shook her head in denial. Hearing her father's name on the Archbishop's tongue had set off an explosion of memories, the soundtrack of her father's steady voice forever repeating: *"for the good of Cyrano..."*

Suddenly it all made sense.

It wasn't their shared dream that she become an advisor to the King. She had been the one to misinterpret that. That was *her* dream. *Her* mistake.

Her father had wanted her to become Queen.

The room spun as her perspective on her entire relationship with her father shifted.

His insistence on her studying, his absolute refusal when it came to the subject of dating... His incessant litany of, *"Cyrano is counting on you..."*

He had meant it literally.

The familiar phrase morphed into a menacing phantom swirling around her mind, taunting her as everything she'd ever known about the world went up in flames.

The King knelt, and everyone in the room followed—except for the Archbishop and Mina.

Mina stood frozen.

The Archbishop whispered, "Kneel," and she

knelt, her obedience to a direct order automatic even through her shock.

The Archbishop continued with the ceremony. "When you rise, you rise together as King and Queen of Cyrano. Joined in marriage for the betterment of the nation."

And if we stay down here?

The thought bubbled up in Mina's mind—a deranged joke as her world ended.

The King stood, capturing her elbow his hand with a secure grip, drawing her up beside him.

So much for that, she thought wistfully.

The Archbishop bowed to them, the movement acknowledging them as co-monarchs. The King released Mina's arm to embrace the Archbishop and then lead the older man out.

Mina stared after them, absurd thoughts bouncing around her mind like senseless pinballs: *I was married by the Archbishop of Cyrano... Papa would have been so proud... Papa...*

There was a neon sign in her mind, flashing in bright, desperate alarm.

Her father had married her off. To the King.

An arranged marriage. People didn't do that anymore.

She was a scientist, not a queen.

Her knees buckled, but the King, having returned to the dais, once again steadied her, casting her a frosty glare as he did so.

She turned away from the glare, desperate for something else to focus on, knowing on some level that she couldn't escape, but looking for a route nonetheless.

Again, the King read her mind. "There's no way out."

She shook her head. "There has to be. An annulment. A divorce."

He gave a firm negative with a shake of his head. "It is an edict of the King."

"You're the King."

"I wasn't then. There is no getting out of it. I have exhausted every possibility."

His words stung, even though she was just as desperate for answers.

"This can't be real," she said. "Cyrano is a modern European nation."

As if he were arguing with a toddler, the King's eyelids fluttered closed, and a small sound of exasperation slipped from his lips. "We are. And, like in many modern, *civilized* nations, it is easier to put a law on the books than it is to get it off. Though it pains me to admit it, breaking our betrothal would require a constitutional amendment."

"But you're the King."

His eyes narrowed, a different kind of disappointment entering them. "A king is not above the law. I shudder to think of the counsel you would

have provided as advisor, given that I have to remind you of that fact."

She would have thought that by this point in the
day she would be numb to something so minor as
a casually thrown verbal barb. Instead, his words
cut right to her heart. Hadn't she been thinking
along the same lines about him just moments before?

Before they were married.

"I would never suggest that." She didn't bother
to keep the snap out of her voice. They were married now, after all. She added sarcastically, "Forgive the implication. I'm not at my best. It's not
every day that I am arrested to attend my own
surprise wedding."

Something that might have been compassion
flashed across his eyes, but it was gone before
she could be sure. When he spoke, he said, "Obviously we will go over terms more formally in
the coming weeks, but in the immediacy of today
know this: out of respect for my father, you will
be Queen, with all the associated rights and requirements. That includes a private guard, access to the Queen's suites in the palace, and an
annual salary. Planning and hosting the Queen's
Ball will be your first official duty, and it will
also serve as your debut."

"But that's just two weeks away."

"As I mentioned, it took us longer to locate you than anticipated."

Mina almost laughed. He made it sound as if it was her fault. The only reason she held back a snort was the fear that she would deteriorate into mad cackling if she let it out.

Cyranese custom held that the Queen hosted an annual ball, inviting the entire aristocracy of the island, as well as Members of Parliament, representatives from media outlets, and other illustrious members of society to attend. The tradition had begun a century before—one savvy queen's method of diverting angry lords from violence—but had not taken place in the two years since King Alden's death. The first year the widowed Queen had been too deep in mourning. The second year Zayn had been crowned and the country no longer had a queen.

Traditionally, the ball took place on Queen's Day—two weeks away.

Mina had never planned a party in her life.

Again, the unbelievability of this narrative struck Mina.

A person didn't go from being ordinary one moment to being Queen the next. The Archbishop had conducted the ceremony, but there had been no judge present, no license signed. Surely even the King needed a license and a judge for a marriage to be legal?

But the King had moved on.

"Your guards will be..." he scanned the row of guards "...Moustafa and d'Tierrza."

Two blue-clad figures stepped forward. Both were women. One wore her long brown hair pulled back into a braid nearly as tight and controlled as Mina's. The other sported a swoopy silver-blond pixie cut.

The blonde guard's voice was a low rasp, infused with humor, as she executed a bow and came up saying, "Your Royal Majesty..."

Without missing a beat, the other woman followed, and Mina found herself nodding to them with a genuine smile on her face, amused and slightly grateful at their military manner. It reminded her of her father.

Her father who had secretly arranged her marriage.

Mina pushed the thought away. She wasn't ready to untangle that knot quite yet.

Instead, she focused on the women in front of her.

The blonde woman's name was revealing. The d'Tierrzas were one of the oldest aristocratic families on the island. The family was currently headed by a daughter, the mother scandalously passed over in the father's will, who was infamous for her scandalous appointment to the Royal Guard.

And now she was Mina's guard.

"There are several other matters we need to discuss…" the King's voice cut into Mina's thoughts "…but that will have to wait. I have an appointment. Your guards will escort you to your rooms."

He spoke as if he were working through a to-do list, rather than parting from his new bride. He was so casual about it all that Mina wondered if he had always expected his marriage to be like this—sudden, rushed, and painful.

For once, however, he seemed to be unaware of her train of thought, continuing with, "Meet me in my office tomorrow at eight a.m. We will go over the rest."

Then he was leaving, with the rest of the guards pouring out after him.

Now she was alone with her new guards the small chapel felt colder, the emptiness of the space more profound for its lack of the King.

Her husband.

Mina shivered.

"Your Majesty?" Moustafa asked.

It took Mina a moment to realize the woman was addressing her. When she did, she grimaced. "Please, call me Mina."

The woman nodded. "Mina. Would you like us to escort you to your rooms?"

"If by that you mean my apartment in the city,

that would be wonderful. Can you do that?" Despite everything, she couldn't keep the wistful thread of hope out of her voice.

D'Tierrza laughed out loud. "You certainly deserve it. But we can't—at least not until we've swept and secured the premises." She added the last with a wink.

Mina felt an answering smile grow on her own face as she took a closer look at the other woman. D'Tierrza's rich alto voice and confident demeanor, coupled with her creamy skin and line-free face, as well as the startling clarity of her sapphire-blue eyes, were completely at odds with the danger coiled in her frame. The woman was beautiful—but Mina got the distinct impression that that fact didn't matter to her in the least.

Moustafa had her own stern beauty, with her dark coloring and angular bone structure. Her face was all high cheekbones and slashing brows, and it suited her perfectly. Her surname was common, and she lacked the insouciant ease the island's aristocracy seemed born with. Both facts confirmed the impression that she had made it to the palace the same way Mina had: through hard work and a fierce refusal to give up.

Her guards would make good friends in the palace.

Accepting that, if nothing else, Mina said, "Please lead the way."

Moustafa and d'Tierrza turned, and Mina followed them out of the chapel.

The hallways they took her through were dim and quiet, clearly not open to the public. Low-wattage bulbs provided just enough light throughout, and beneath them the marble floors sparkled.

"These are the residential corridors. You'll eventually figure them all out," d'Tierrza said after the they'd taken a third turn. "They're the fastest way to travel the palace and the grounds and are well guarded and surveilled."

Mina almost laughed. It would be some time before the security of the premises became a concern of hers. She was a scientist, not a dignitary. Or she had been.

After a long walk, they finally stopped in front of another wooden door and Mina flinched. Her day at the palace had become a nightmare of Monty Hall problems.

So what monstrosity lurks behind door number three? she wondered as she pushed it open.

Only this time is wasn't a nightmare. It was a paradise.

The room was all wide-open ivory walls and floors and creamy marble. There were several open archways leading into other spaces, all of which encircled a large sunken sitting room that was comfortably appointed with plush furniture. The upholstery was smooth buff suede, and there were pillows and throw blankets everywhere one might want to reach for one.

As Mina entered, d'Tierrza stopped her with a hand on the shoulder. "For the Queen's Ball, call Roz Chastain. She'll take you because you're new. Let her have her way on everything."

She took out a pen and paper and scribbled a number down.

Mina nodded, a sense of relief penetrating her for the first time since she had learned she had landed the Parliament interview months ago.

"Thank you."

D'Tierrza grinned. "My money is on you. I've never seen anyone affect him like you do. He completely lost his cool—and that can only be good for him."

With those enigmatic words, she gently nudged Mina inside before taking her position outside the door.

Moustafa took her position as well, leaving Mina to wander in and out of each room.

The wing included a bedroom, a bathroom suite with a tiled hot tub, a large-windowed office with a stunning view, and an enormous balcony overlooking the sea.

The bed was lush, and freshly made with bright linens and fluffy pillows. The towels were the thickest she had ever felt, and a gorgeous robe and slipper set was hanging outside the double-headed waterfall shower.

Interestingly, while the suite was stunning—indeed, the most elegant accommodation Mina had ever been in—there were signs that the wing had not been updated in at least a few decades. Rotary phones graced the side tables in the bedroom and the sitting room, three nineteen-fifties era television sets that Mina was sure would not connect to Cyrano's digital cable network rested on sideboards in multiple places, and there wasn't a computer in sight.

All it needed was a laptop and decent Wi-Fi signal, though, and it would make the perfect location for a research sabbatical.

Not for her, of course.

After the fiasco of her arrest and then her firing, her career was ruined. Academia was quick to condemn and slow to forgive. The only thing for her to do was fade into the shadows quietly.

A feat that would be more challenging now that she was apparently Queen.

Her academic reputation was tarnished.

She was Queen of Cyrano.

It was her wedding day.

She was alone.

Walking into the bedroom, weary in a way she never imagined she could be, she collapsed on the bed without taking her clothes off or loosening her braid. The SWAT team had done a good enough job of that last bit.

She hadn't harbored many of the fantasies common to young girls. Weddings, babies—none of that—but she had still vaguely imagined that she'd marry. Probably not until the autumn of her life, and likely only then to a warmly regarded colleague. But she'd pictured it. Even in that tame picture, though, she hadn't gone to bed alone on her wedding night.

Rolling over onto her back, she stared at the bright ceiling, no longer able to hold back the wave of emotion.

She was the Queen of Cyrano and her greatest dream was a warm pile of smoking ash.

For the first time since her father died, Mina cried herself to sleep.

CHAPTER TWO

SOME MEN WERE driven by passion, acting on their instincts without thought or strategy. Much to his late father's chagrin, Zayn Darius d'Argonia, the youngest ever King of Cyrano, was not that kind of man.

It was the old man's own fault, though. After all, he had been the one to raise a young prince with an ironclad sense of self-reliance and an unwavering commitment to forging his own path. Early on in his life, he had decided that his was the path of careful study and planning.

To give his father credit, he had, on most issues, steadfastly supported Zayn in whatever approach he chose, saying, *"Each man is his own. It does the world no good to try to walk the path of another."*

His father had believed this self-reliance was a vital characteristic for a king. Of course, neither of them had imagined that Zayn would become King so soon. Nor that, in that transition, his inner compass would be the only thing that saved the country from near governmental collapse, economic depression, and an attempted coup in the immediate and ugly aftermath of the King's assassination and the ascendance of a young, inexperienced monarch to the throne.

But any self-flagellation for lack of foresight on the matter was a pointless waste of time—a luxury a working king could not afford.

Some believed that Parliament ran things. They were mistaken.

Cyrano's monarchy had given its people a powerful voice through their elected officials, and more power still through the Parliament-selected advisory council, but the royal family had retained control and rule of the country—through centuries and countless plots against them.

Zayn would not be the one to jeopardize that— not through poor planning, not through acting rashly, and not through marriage.

And that was just one of the many reasons the shock of his betrothal still stung.

Filling the position of Queen was to have been one of his most potent bargaining chips—a lucrative lure to play to Cyrano's strategic advantage.

The woman who would be Queen had to be cut from a particular cloth—intelligent, quick-thinking, compassionate, determined, unflappable, steel-coated, perfectly presented, and always poised. And she needed to bring something of real value to the Crown—money, trade, connections…something tangible.

She could not be common. She could not be unfashionable. She couldn't let her feelings show in her beautiful green-gold eyes every time someone was frank with her.

His greatest bargaining chip was now a virtual throwaway, offering nothing advantageous to the nation and burdening him with a softhearted academic unprepared for the sharp edges of public life in the process. That his father had been the one to hamstring him like this made it all the worse.

It didn't make any sense. Up to the very end, his father had done everything he could to support him.

Zayn had already considered the obvious—that Mina's family had somehow blackmailed the late King—but it didn't pan out.

While his father had been no angel, Zayn was sure there were no skeletons in his closet so monstrous that he would sacrifice his son. Nothing had mattered more to King Alden than his family. It didn't add up—especially given the old King's feelings on marriage.

While he was alive, marriage had been the one point of disagreement between them.

Never one to keep his opinions to himself,

Alden had tried his damnedest to turn his son around to his thinking.

"Your Queen will be your greatest helpmeet and partner. She will be the difference between a legacy of success or failure. Finding her, falling in love—and soon—that is your most important duty."

Fresh from his second year at university, and riding high on the thrill of finding his passion in the philosophy and study of governance, Zayn had merely rolled his eyes at his father's hyperbole.

His father had persisted. *"I'm serious, son. I don't want to hear any more of this 'strategic alliance once you take the throne' nonsense. I want you to fall in love, and fast."*

"Regardless of this mystery woman's status or fitness to rule?" Zayn had replied, not bothering to rein in the sarcasm in his voice.

King Alden's eyes had briefly darted away that day, and Zayn had counted the point as his victory, but now he knew better. His father hadn't met his eyes that day because he had been playing the hypocrite.

And therein lay the rub.

Why go to the trouble to wax on about love and marriage when he'd already given his son away?

Perhaps his father had been more strategic than Zayn had given him credit. Maybe he'd owed someone a favor for his good fortune, and Zayn had been the repayment. That kind of *quid pro quo* was the norm amongst the ruling set. The logic was clean.

But Zayn didn't believe it for a minute.

Logical though it might be, the idea was uncharitable to the man his father had been, and about as far out of character and respect to the relationship they'd shared as this whole betrothal fiasco was in the first place.

Whatever the circumstances had been, his father had not conned his way onto the throne. King Alden and Queen Barbara's had been a great love. The intensity of it had gone so far as to be a frequent distraction from rule, in Zayn's opinion. But his father had insisted that their passion set the tone for the nation, energizing its transition from a European backwater into the next most-desired off-the-beaten-path destination.

It was hard to believe that the same man would—either strategically, or under threat— bargain his son away.

So how in God's name had he ended up married to a stranger? And why had his father kept the betrothal from him?

The betrothal agreement was dated just weeks before Zayn's birth, witnessed by the former Archbishop, Henry Innocence, and signed by both Zayn's and Mina's fathers. Curiously, their mothers' signatures were absent.

With nothing more to offer than that, the current Archbishop, Samuel, had raised his palms pacifyingly and said, "I'm sorry, Your Majesty. The late Archbishop made no note about the betrothal in his diary entries. I scoured the entire year's worth myself."

Nothing about the situation made sense, and no one could explain. Indeed, logic had taken its leave of the situation from the moment Zayn had approached Archbishop Samuel with his list of prospective brides.

Each of those women would have brought something of advantage to Cyrano.

Daphne Xianopolis came with access to excellent Mediterranean Sea trade routes. Françoise La Guerre was a princess in her own right, and marriage to her would have opened up the potential for stronger diplomatic ties to continental Europe. And Yu Yan Ma would have been the most fabulous prize. Connection to her father would have given him power enough to propel Cyrano into the world of international trade.

Zayn had merely intended the Archbishop to vet the list for any potential religious challenges before he made began making approaches. Instead, he'd learned that he was otherwise engaged.

"What do you mean, I'm 'already taken?'"
Zayn had demanded.

The Archbishop had smiled, as if the situation were a delightful joke, and repeated, "You are affianced, Your Majesty. You have been since before you were born."

"That's impossible!"

But it had not been impossible. The archbishop had shown him the official document, signed, witnessed, and filed—binding in every way— and Zayn had been forced to acknowledge the truth.

Dr. Amina Aldaba would bring nothing of value to Cyrano. As far as he could discern, she was nobody. She came from simple people of Moorish descent. Her father had been eighth generation Cyranese and had first a soldier, then a farmer—not the kind of man who entered his unborn child into a royal betrothal.

Like all natural-born Cyranese men, her father had served in the military for mandatory service at eighteen. Unlike most, he had re-enlisted for another three terms of service, earning enough money to purchase a small villa at the edge of the city. City permit records showed that he had then converted two courtyards into farm plots and taken to life as a vendor at the city's famous daily market. A few years later he'd married Elke

Meyer—a woman who had arrived in Cyrano on a student visa.

The couple had married in the courthouse and had one child. They'd lived as a family until the father's death thirteen years later. Nowhere in that timeline was there any record of their family's path crossing with the royal line. Not in service, not in friendship—nothing that would suggest a closeness that might brook the future joining of their families that was constitutionally binding.

And so Zayn had Dr. Amina Aldaba for his Queen—a woman who had spent her life absorbed in academia, developing no practical skills for queenship.

She would need to learn everything from scratch, and there was no way he could keep her out of the limelight long enough for her to master the ins and outs of public life. Undoubtedly, she would embarrass the Crown along the way.

With her over-starched headmistress aesthetic and easily ruffled feathers, it was obvious she was better suited to that scientific advisory position on the council than the throne. At least in that role she would have had something to recommend her. Zayn had scoured her research and found her work insightful. He could see why Parliament had approved her interview.

In the role of scientific advisor, she would have been perfect.

There was nothing to recommend her for the role of Queen.

A protest against the thought rose from some vague, primal part of his mind. She didn't exactly have *nothing* to recommend her. That much was clear, even with the atrocious packaging.

Her eyes were astonishing—a shade of green that Zayn had never seen before, falling somewhere between that of the sage that grew in the dry upper reaches of Cyrano's hills and the new spring grasses that grew in the meadowlands.

And her gaze had depth—enough that it was easy to fall into it, like a moss-lined crevasse in a mountain forest.

Her skin, too—a satiny brown that glowed warm and bright wherever the light touched it—was notable. Smooth and clear, it virtually demanded to be caressed.

Like her skin, her hair, too, hinted at softness, even shellacked and tightly braided as it had been. The color of her hair had reminded Zayn of the brown beaches of the island palace, its chocolatey brown and natural highlights calling to his mind the island's long stretches of pristine coastline, dappled with dancing ribbons of sunlight streaming through the woods.

Her eyebrows were a shade darker than her hair, thick and fierce over her magnificent eyes.

Her coloring was that of the Mediterranean

landscape, come to vibrant life in the form of woman. He sensed that the rest of her—everything she hid beneath her over-sized and over-starched office wear—would be just as vibrant and bountiful.

There were hints of it even with the camouflage. Her lips were full and defined even naked of lipstick, as they had been. They were naturally rose-colored, lending her mouth a naughty allure that she didn't even bother to hide.

Her utter lack of effort to accentuate her beauty only seemed to emphasize the truth of it.

Her nose was straight-bridged, with a rounded tip, lending her expressive face an element of forthrightness that offset any urge to write her off as merely pretty.

Instead, she was earnest. Pure. *Untasted*.

That last thought was unlike him.

And, at thirty-six years old, it was highly unlikely that she remained untasted.

But, shoving that thought to the side, he was willing to acknowledge that it wasn't fair to say she brought *nothing* the table. She would be lovely when adequately dressed.

Unfortunately, "lovely" was usually only as exciting and useful as the time it took to secure a taste of it. "Lovely" wasn't reason enough for most common men to marry, let alone a king.

Zayn glanced up at the wall clock in his office

to note that she was five minutes late. She didn't even have the sense to respect the demands on his time. They had a great deal they needed to discuss concerning the terms of their marriage and he didn't have all day.

He watched the ticking passage of another two minutes before she walked in, head high.

As it had been the day before, her armor—or, more accurately, her schoolmarm disguise—was in place: controlled braid, no-nonsense posture, and a direct stare. Though by now, day two, her suit was beginning to lose its crisp edges. This morning she looked more like a wilting librarian than a roughed-up rigid professor.

Zayn gave her a once-over before saying, "Your clothing is ridiculous. You'll need to work on that."

Hurt flickered across her gaze, but she schooled her expression.

She'll need to work on that, too, he thought.

A queen needed thick skin.

Taking her in, he mentally sighed. Her eyes were slightly puffy and swollen—a telltale sign that she had cried the night before. A queen needed to be prepared for long, thankless days and constant smiling, for being bombarded with hate and never revealing whether she was hurt, tired, ill, or angry. Mina might as well have been a projector screen for the way she broadcasted her feelings to the world.

Zayn added, "As Queen, you are expected to dress at the height of fashion and always be well presented. You have a budget for that express purpose, as it is considered part and parcel of your royal duties."

Her cheeks darkened but she made no comment to his remark, so he gestured for her to sit down at the desk across from him. The desk had been his father's before his, and his grandfather's before that. The very room itself had been the King's office since the palace's construction.

And now it was his.

Mina sat, looking around the office as she did so. For once, her expression did not give away her thoughts. Her posture was ramrod-straight as she sat at the edge of the chair, legs primly pressed together, hands in her lap.

It was a small blessing, and, observing her, he could at least find no fault with her there. When his eyes finally moved back up to meet hers, she cleared her throat and opened her mouth.

"I'm not the Queen. We're not married."

The words, abrupt and inelegant, hung in the air between them.

Zayn closed his eyes and took a breath before answering. "We are."

It wasn't that he hadn't been expecting her to

say something along those lines. He'd merely hoped she would be smart enough to understand that if there had been a way out of the situation, he would have found it.

She shook her head. "There was nothing legal about that ceremony."

"I assure you, our union is legal and binding."

"That's ridiculous," Mina insisted. "You didn't even know who I was the day before yesterday."

"Not true. I've known who you are for exactly three weeks."

She looked taken aback by that fact, but pressed on. "You can't force a woman to marry you. You said it yourself: 'The King is not above the law.'"

"No. But fathers can apparently still force their children to marry."

"So, this is real?"

She sounded so desolate he was tempted to take pity on her—but she was the Queen now, and making it easy on her wouldn't be doing her any favors.

So he didn't, instead saying, "It is. So, if we may continue?" He inclined his head toward the stack of forms sitting at her right hand. "There are several legal statements you must sign. You are to select one to three, but no more, causes to champion. These will then inform your outreach activities."

Her expression suggested that he'd grown another head, but she said nothing so he continued.

"Your attendance is expected at all official state functions. A personal secretary has been assigned to you to manage your calendar, your discretionary budgets, and personal affairs."

Zayn noted that her color was fading, but she remained upright, present, and attentive. It would do. He sensed there was more going on inside, but overnight she seemed to have managed to gain some control over her constant emoting.

At least she was a quick study. She would need to be. There were those who would use her every emotion against her, and he wouldn't always be around to protect her.

"Your diplomatic functions will include acting as royal hostess, overseeing entrainment for visiting dignitaries, and representing Cyrano whenever abroad."

At this, she brightened, once again broadcasting her feelings, transparent as glass. He'd given her credit too soon.

"Politically, should anything happen to me, you are to take my place as ruler, working closely with the advisory council—"

She sucked in a pained breath at his mention of the council, and he felt another twinge of regret. Not for firing her from the position. That had been a given. The Queen did not have a seat on the advisory council. But he could find sympathy for her obvious disappointment.

Continuing, he said, "In readiness for such an emergency, you are to keep abreast of the status and scope of my duties as well as your own. This is considered a royal duty, and you will be allotted time for review in your official schedule."

Here was another duty she felt an affinity for, judging from the ease she radiated.

For the thousandth time he wondered why his father had chosen her—and for the thousandth time he brushed the thought away.

Speculation was a waste of his time.

"Other duties will be assigned as they arise, but you will be informed well in advance. I mentioned that you would receive a wardrobe budget. In addition to that, you will receive an administrative budget and an annual salary. You will get three months of vacation per year, and six months of maternity leave—"

Mina made a choking sound in the back of her throat, and the energy in the room took on a new edge.

They had not yet discussed heirs.

Heirs—or at least the attempt—would be one of her essential duties as Queen. It was literally spelled out in the position's description.

As Zayn took her in now, a burst of color masquerading as a deflating cardboard box, he was surprised to feel heat stirring in his gut.

Unlike the women on his list, Mina bore none of the traits he found attractive in a woman. She was tall, whereas he liked petite, serious whereas he valued humor, and, he suspected, she was curvaceous under her suit—more like a proud Valkyrie than a woman with the willowy frame he preferred.

His father couldn't have selected a more inappropriate woman for him had he tried.

And yet...

Zayn cleared his throat. "Out of consideration for our heirs, and the continuation of the d'Argonia line, both parties are prohibited from extramarital relations until the union has produced three children who have lived past the age of five."

Mina's face, having darkened when he began, was a mortified mask of purple by the time he'd finished.

"That's oddly specific," she squeaked.

He would have called it distasteful, but essentially he agreed. This conversation was crude. All this information was included in the marriage contract, usually reviewed by each party privately before the wedding. However, there was nothing usual about this marriage.

"Once we have produced the requisite number

of heirs, we are free to explore or return to other relationships." He found himself frowning as he spoke, oddly as insulted by the idea of Mina taking a lover as he'd been intrigued by the idea of producing an heir with her.

"Perhaps we can take it slow when it comes to heirs," she suggested, her voice coming out scratchy and uneven. Her cheeks were still red-tinged, and she had pushed her seat back, away from the opposite side of the desk.

Unbidden, he had a distinct impression of innocence from her, followed by a strangely conflicted dual surge of interest and frustration. He chose to focus on the frustration. Training a prudish virgin scholar in bed was the last thing he wanted.

The answering rush of heat to his groin, however, said otherwise.

Ignoring it, he nodded at Mina. "Certainly. Everything is spelled out in the marriage agreement." He tapped the thickly bound stack of papers on the desk. "Copies are filed here, as well as in your own office and with the state office. I mentioned the Queen's Ball yesterday... As your first official duty, your work on it must reflect the quality and standards of the Crown. The royal steward will inform you if you've achieved that. Now, if you don't have any questions, you may take your leave."

The phrasing was open, but his dismissal clear.

Instead of taking her leave, though, Mina opened her mouth.

"I've certainly got questions. Let's say that I believe this impossible situation is irreversible, for the sake of this conversation. If that's the case, what about my things? I have an apartment and a car in the city, as well as a storage unit filled with my research. My laptop and phone were confiscated outside Parliament. I will need those returned if I—"

Zayn held up a hand to stop her. "You will be given new encrypted devices, and your belongings are being seen to by palace staff as we speak. Your car has been donated to charity. As Queen, you will not need a vehicle—and you are, in fact, not allowed to drive."

"That's absurd!" Mina protested.

"Regardless, it is true."

"I have rights as a citizen of Cyrano."

Zayn shook his head, ruefully. "You are no longer a citizen of Cyrano. You are the Queen of Cyrano."

"And if I refuse?"

"There is no refusing."

"It's not right."

Zayn stared at her for a moment before slightly inclining his head. "I agree. But it *is*. And it is more important than you or I."

Mina frowned. "Your cavalier response to an obvious injustice leaves a bit to be desired."

"As does your reaction to the acquiring of new and unwanted responsibility. It seems we both have room for growth." Zayn's voice was even, but no less cutting for its collegiate tone.

Her green eyes narrowed. "Do not presume to know the first thing about me, *Your Royal Majesty*."

She was right. The fact that her words were valid only added to the acid sting of them. He knew nothing about her—and yet she was his wife.

"I do not. Neither, however, should you make assumptions about me. Aren't we lucky that it appears we will have many years together to learn?"

And how does any of this prove your point, Father? he wondered.

How in the world did marrying him to a stranger prove how urgently important it was that he find a wife to love and cherish? His father had contradicted every single one of his words to his son about love and marriage before he'd even said them in the first place, betrothing him to a stranger and never giving him the chance to come to know and love her.

Zayn had at least known the women on his list socially. Some he had known a bit more. That had to make a stronger foundation upon which to build love than no knowledge whatsoever.

And if a love match had been King Alden's hope for his son, why had he taken the choice from him? If he had truly believed a partner must be a helpmeet, why hadn't he prepared this woman for her future role? Or even informed her of it, for that matter?

Unfortunately, there were more questions than answers, and no time to spend on them—especially now that he had a stubborn and inept queen sitting in his office.

It didn't matter that the issue burned in him all the more for being the one subject that he and his father had never seen eye-to-eye on. No. All that mattered was the future of Cyrano.

And Cyrano would weather this—just as it had endured the loss of its King, two years of turmoil, and a century of war and technological transformation before that.

That kind of continuity was more significant than his feelings, his father's and his wife's combined.

Turning back to the woman across the desk from him, he noted that while she had no retort for him, neither did she appear to be any closer to leaving.

"Is there anything else, Dr. Aldaba?" he asked.

Her color was high and bright, but not the dusky rose of her earlier embarrassment, and she looked as if she was casting about for a reason to linger. Frustration poured off her, and Zayn was momentarily comforted by the return of his ease in reading her.

Finally, she said, "When can I expect my new personal devices?"

She was grasping for power and control over something, and they both knew it, but instead of irritating him, the pointless effort stirred something like pity inside him.

He glanced up at the clock. "They should be waiting for you in your office, along with your new secretary, by the time you return there."

Again, the dismissal was blunt—and again she stayed where she was.

"You're certain there's nothing we can do?" she asked after another long pause.

He almost didn't hear the quiet question. The note of defeat and vulnerability in her voice called out to him, but he reminded himself that pity did her no favors. A queen had to be impenetrable.

"I am certain. Now, I suggest you return to your office. Please select your causes soon, and inform your secretary so that we may update the royal website. And, please, for the love of God, assign someone to your wardrobe immediately."

As he'd intended, she pursed her lips and narrowed her eyes into outraged green slits. Gone was the air of fragility, replaced with the heat of anger and the spark of determination he'd seen her muster so many times in their brief interactions.

She stood stiffly and he almost smiled, relieved to see the fire radiating from her. She was going to need fire like that if she was going to make it as Queen.

CHAPTER THREE

"AND PLEASE, FOR the love of God, assign someone to your wardrobe..."

A week and a half later, standing in front of her new closet, staring at the same old four black cocktail dresses she owned, the King's words still stung.

It was the morning of the ball and, while she might not have taken his advice in the time since their meeting, she had taken d'Tierrza's.

Like a fairy godmother, Roz Chastain had turned out to be everything Mina hadn't known she needed.

Roz wore a uniform that consisted of a long-sleeved boat-necked black shirt with black skinny jeans and leopard print loafers. Her mind was as sharp as a sword, and—a fact Mina could personally attest to—her tongue even sharper.

Mina could scarcely believe the day of the ball had arrived as she settled on the sleeveless dress. The dress's design was plain, but suitable, as were the simple black ballet flats she would wear with it. Both had served her well through years of parties, publication celebrations, and galas.

With the task of choosing her ensemble complete, she glanced at the clock. It was early—just past seven in the morning—and, after Roz's efforts and hers, she had the whole of the rest of the day to relax before the big event.

Grabbing her mug of tea from the side table where it rested, she made her way onto the large wrap-around balcony of the Queen's Wing and considered trying her mother's phone again.

Since her father's death, her mother had run the family farm business on her own, ferociously protecting Mina's study time by refusing to allow her to help—even if that meant working from dawn to dusk to maintain the thriving business and the house in support of the dreams of her daughter and her late husband.

In anticipation of how busy Mina would be, preparing for her parliamentary interview, her mother had taken a rare trip back to Germany. They were to reconnect when she returned in late summer.

But what would she say to her? *Hi, Mom. I got married.*

She would be heartbroken—not just because she had missed one of the most important major milestones of her daughter's life, but also for the same reason Mina was. Her father had kept this secret from both of them. Of that fact Mina was of no doubt. There was no way her mother would have kept her betrothal from her. She knew her too well to leave her that unprepared. And now, in addition to swallowing her daughter's marriage and becoming Queen, her mother would also have to reckon with her husband's great secret.

It wasn't something Mina was willing to do over the phone. No, it was better to wait until her return and to break the news gently, in person.

So instead of calling her mom she took a deep breath of sea air.

Overlooking the stunning Mediterranean, the smooth architecture of the balcony was timelessly elegant, although it was a bit chilly. Mina wore a pair of slouchy boyfriend jeans, wool socks, sandals, and a knit sweater, and still the sea breezes found their way to her skin.

Her long braid, dangling down the center of her back now, had loosened over the past nine days. It was just one of many signals that her life as a scholar was over.

The thought brought an ache to her chest.

Looking out to sea, she wondered what, if anything, her colleagues had learned of her humiliation.

The ball was to be her debut as Queen, so no information about her identity had been publicly released. Neither had she found anything about her dramatic parliamentary interview online, or in any of the city's newspapers. Not that she had had much time to look, ensconced with Roz in event-planning as she had been.

Their efforts had been well worth it, though. It was amazing what could be accomplished in a short amount of time when one had limitless funds and access to a ruthless genius event-planner.

A knock on the door startled a jump out of her, and tea sloshed over her sweater sleeve. It served her right. She had been about to lose herself in thoughts about the King. It was enough that he was devastatingly handsome. She didn't need to compound the situation by developing Stockholm syndrome.

Moving as quickly as she could, while also steadying the mug, Mina hurried to the door and opened it to find Roz standing in the hallway.

Without a word, the older woman pushed the door open wide and Mina to one side.

"Out of the way, dear," she rasped.

Mina frowned. The other woman's behavior was not unusual, but it was unexpected. As far as Mina had understood, they'd had no plans to see each other until the ball tonight.

A young woman also dressed all in black had followed Roz into the room, wheeling a large beauty salon chair and vanity unit in front of her. Another woman sporting an extreme asymmetrical haircut and a color block dress followed. A heartbeat later, a bald man with a salt-and-pepper beard, thick black glasses, and a thin gray sweater entered. The last to come, and the shortest of the lot, was a woman with a face so perfect it looked like a painting. She shut the door behind her.

Mina looked around the suddenly crowded room. "Roz. Everyone... To what do I owe the pleasure of your company?"

Before answering, Roz conversed with the first young woman about where to place the salon chair. Then she replied, "We're here to fix you, my dear."

Mina laughed. "I wasn't aware that I was broken—but, thank you, Roz."

Roz gifted her with a stare utterly devoid of patience and, much like the vacuum of space, of life itself. Roz did not like to repeat herself.

"I did not put together the event of the year in a single week to have it fizzle out at the finale."

Mina set her tea on a side table and wrapped her arms around herself protectively. "And how does that relate to me?" she asked.

Roz's eyebrow inched up, setting off alarms in Mina's head. She had seen that look before.

"You are the finale, dear, and as it is now you simply won't do."

Mina frowned. "What's wrong with me?"

"Nothing. Other than the fact you plan to wear a depressingly square department store cocktail dress to my ball."

Heat came to Mina's cheeks even as she shook her head in denial. The dress hadn't come from a department store. It was from a boutique that had been going out of business. And it was not square.

Reading her mind, Roz said, "Everything you wear is square. Off with it all. Put this on." She held out an ivory silk robe.

Shoulders slumped, Mina took the robe and turned toward her bathroom with a sigh.

Roz stopped her with a commanding click of her tongue. "Where are you going?"

Mina turned around slowly, feeling as guilty as if she had tried to disobey her mother. She winced. "To change?" she said, the question in her voice acknowledging that it was obviously the wrong answer.

"Not in the bathroom." Roz shook her head. "Right here. We need measurements."

The woman with the asymmetrical hair nodded.

Mina shook her head. "No."

Roz tsked. "Don't be stubborn, Mina. You don't have anything that everyone in this room hasn't seen a million times before."

The woman with the perfect face smiled encouragingly, adding in a soft, wispy voice, "It's true."

With her inherent modesty now being repre-
sented as immaturity—at least in the eyes of this
roomful of strangers who were waiting to see
her naked—Mina gritted her teeth and pulled
her sweater over her head. She followed it with
the rest of her clothes, until she stood shivering
in the bright morning light wearing nothing but
her underwear.

"Good figure," the woman with the perfect
face commented.

"Bad underwear," asymmetrical haircut added.

Mina's cheeks heated uncomfortably.

Roz agreed. "Horrible. Get rid of them."

Mina started to shake her head, but realized
there was no point. Roz always won in the end.

Face aflame, she quickly removed her undergarments until she stood naked in the room. The
woman with asymmetrical hair darted over and
began taking measurements, calling out numbers
to the young woman in black, who took notes.

When she'd finished, Mina quickly shrugged
the robe over her nakedness, just before the
woman gave her a little push toward the bald man
and the salon chair. Then she took the notes from
the younger woman and hurried out of the room.

Staring at the chair, and the man who stood behind it, Mina heard her practical German mother's voice rising in her mind: *"Never trust a bald
hairstylist."*

But there was no getting out of it.

Sucking in a deep breath, Mina sat in the chair.

The man spun a cape around her and secured it at her neck. In one swift motion, he slid a pair of scissors out of the pocket of the apron at his waist and cut the elastic that held the end of her braid.

Mina reached up with lightning speed to place her hand on his wrist. Turning to meet his eyes, she said, "Please don't cut too much off. I've been growing it for over twenty years…"

Since her father had died.

The man grimaced, as if her statement explained everything, and then waved her words away with little flicks of his hand. "Don't worry, sweetheart. I'm going to make you look divine."

And then he moved behind her and made his first cut into her bone-dry hair.

Her stomach knotted as he worked. No one had ever cut her hair dry before.

She winced at every thick slice, each one a visceral reminder that scissors were now shearing their way through years' worth of growth in curls that were slow to grow and quick to frizz.

She took a deep breath.

It was only hair.

Hair that hung past her rear end when it was wet.

Hair that she hadn't cut since her father had died because he had seen the stubborn curls as a reflection of her inner strength and determination.

Her heart squeezed, but she didn't move in the chair. She was strong enough to endure a haircut.

By the time the stylist moved to the front of her head she wasn't so sure.

Not only had he taken off inches and inches of length all over her head, he'd done the unthinkable for a curly woman—added multiple chunky layers. A pained moan bubbled out of Mina's throat, and her eyes teared as he continued, oblivious. He completed his massacre with a flourish and two swipes of his scissors, saving the worst horror for last: a set of frizzy, puffy bangs.

He had turned her into a nineteen-eighties poodle.

Then he barked, "Washbowl!"

The girl all in black ran over, pushing a portable sink and that had appeared in the room sometime when Mina wasn't looking. Raising Mina's seat with the foot lever, the man tilted her back and began washing her hair.

The light, fresh aroma of the shampoo, combined with the relaxing pressure of his fingers massaging her scalp, lulled her mind away from the monstrosity he had made of her head.

A haircut is temporary, she mentally repeated to herself.

The mantra was easy enough to believe with her eyes closed and strong hands massaging her skull. When he sat her back up and she heard the distinctive sound of foil crinkling, though, all sense of ease evaporated.

She opened her eyes in time to see him painting a dollop of white cream onto a wet curly clump, and slapping a piece of foil on top of it. He made quick work of a second and a third, before the first squeak escaped the frozen O of Mina's mouth.

Without pausing in his application, he said, "Relax—you'll hardly notice it."

Heart beating rapidly, Mina tried to breathe. She had never colored her hair. She had always heard that color was the death of curls.

In far less time than she felt it should have taken, the stylist had her whole head foiled. He stood back and admired his handiwork while Mina's stomach churned.

Roz smiled. "That's good for now. Someone call for lunch. We will eat and then continue working while the color sets. Time is ticking."

Food arrived moments later, and the group ate efficiently, quietly talking amongst themselves. All except for Mina, who took robotic bites of food and stared woodenly at the clumps of her hair littering the floor.

And then round two began—not with the hairstylist, as Mina had expected, but with the woman with the perfect face.

Upon closer examination, Mina could tell that the woman's visage was the result of careful and precise makeup application. She had used lighter and darker colors to alter the dimensions and shape of her face like an artist with paints on canvas.

"I'm excellent. I know."

The woman's voice was wry when she spoke, and Mina stopped staring long enough to make eye contact. "My apologies," she muttered.

"None needed," the woman said. "Be still."

And then she set to work.

An hour later, she stepped away from Mina and handed her a mirror.

Mina's mouth dropped open at what she saw— only it wasn't her mouth. It was the lush, deep, red-wine–colored mouth of a siren. Or, set against the bronzed sheen of her golden-brown skin, it looked like the mouth of an ancient Egyptian goddess. In that vein, Mina's large hazel eyes were lined in thick black, and her lashes curled and darkened to match. Her eyelids shimmered with shades of gold, drawing out the similar specks floating in the depths of her irises.

She looked…arresting, even with a head full of foils.

The short woman said to the man, "Don't wash any off when you finish her hair. You'll owe me three-hundred and twenty-five crowns' worth of product if you do."

Mina swallowed. Three hundred and twenty-five crowns for one coating of face paint? She had only ever spent that much of money on rare texts when she'd been unable to secure them through the university library.

The man merely snorted before tilting Mina's chair back. His busy hands made quick work of the foils, and soon his strong fingers were once again massaging her head in the sink.

After using another lovely-smelling product in her hair he gave it a light rinse, before tilting her upright and pulling out a strangely shaped hairdryer.

Mina closed her eyes, dreading the frizzy mess her hair would be when he'd finished with her. Her hair did not take well to blow drying.

While he set to work, Roz addressed the room. "Where are the clothes?"

Someone ran off. Mina did not see who it was.

After what felt like a lifetime of blow-drying, two sets of feet shuffled back into the room.

"You give me no time, but I still work miracles."

Mina recognized the lyrical voice of the woman with the asymmetrical haircut.

"Yes. Yes. Get over here. She's ready," Roz rasped.

The man spun Mina in the chair to face Roz.

"Stand," Roz commanded.

Mina did.

The woman handed her undergarments first—though Mina wasn't sure there was enough fabric for the underwear to be considered a garment. An impossibly thin and seamless black thong—a tiny triangle of material—slid on like silk and felt like a cool nothing.

Mina had never worn a thong.

Scholars did not wear thongs.

The woman then reached out her arm for the robe. Mina looked around, frowning. The whole team of five watched expectantly, again with no patience for her modesty. Reluctantly, she shrugged the robe off her shoulders, leaving herself exposed before them, this time topless in nothing but the thong.

The woman crouched in front of Mina with a creamy liquid gold piece of fabric that put a warm glow into the bright room.

As was clearly expected of her, Mina stepped inside its circle.

The woman pulled the garment up over Mina's hips to cover her body.

The fabric was as thin as the thong and softer than a rose petal. It whispered against her skin as the woman fastened the clasp behind her neck. The cut was a very deep halter and the fabric an exquisite silk, clearly of the highest quality. The design was simple, as elegant as it was revealing.

It was virtually backless and fit snugly around her hips and rear before falling gracefully to pool around her feet.

Mina squeaked when the woman's hand darted under the dress to place a small adhesive cone over one nipple. Ignoring her, the woman repeated the process on the other breast and then stepped back to look at her handiwork.

A fierce and prideful light had appeared in the woman's eyes. Roz gave a satisfied nod, and Mina knew that whatever their goal had been, they had achieved it.

"Shoes!" Roz barked.

The girl in black ran over with a pair of elegant pumps in the same gold color as the dress. The heels were three inches, if they were anything, and Mina had never worn anything over an inch and a half.

She sighed. Of *course* there would be heels. She had never quite mastered the balance and the shifting of weight required to walk in heels with any grace. Walking around in these would be a nightmare. But as she wrapped her fingers around their bright red soles and slid her foot inside she was surprised to find them comfortable.

Roz said, "Turn around."

Mina did as she was told, and gasped when she saw the creature that stared at her from the full-length mirror that had been dug up from some-where.

The woman in the mirror was not Dr. Amina Aldaba, only daughter of Ajit and Elke Aldaba. *That* woman wore a severe braid and boxy suits.

The woman in the mirror was an art deco god-dess in a perfectly fitted dress of luminous golden silk. Her skin gleamed a warm brown, as if it had been buffed and polished like a pearl, and her hair exploded around her head and shoulders like a starburst of bouncy hydrated curls, every one defined, their dimension magnified by gor-geous highlights.

She looked like the kind of girl who danced all night and slept through lectures, rather than the sort of girl who had not gone to a single so-cial event during the entire course of her univer-sity studies.

She looked confident and…and busty. Very, very busty.

The low cut of the dress and its snugness around the hips highlighted her figure, rather than hid it, and she fleetingly wondered what King Zayn would think. It was indeed a change from her suit.

When she finally spoke, her voice was a thin croak, pathetic even to her ears. "I'm stunning."

"Of course you are, dear. Would you expect anything less of my grand finale?"

Mina laughed, her eyes glistening, though she would never let a tear fall and mess up her makeup. "Certainly not, Roz," she said.

Roz's team started packing up their tools, and Mina tore her gaze away from a mirror to check the time. The whole process had taken the bulk of the day, but there were still two hours until the ball began.

She tottered over to the chair that sat near the window, overlooking the sea. Her current novel sat on a table beside it. Her thought was that she would not muss herself if she just sat and read, but Roz barked at her even as she began to bend.

"Stop! No sitting. Practice walking instead. We haven't much time to get you proficient. You might look the part, but it will all be for nothing if you fall flat on your face when it is time to take your mask off."

Roz deserved an award for her way with words, but Mina only snorted.

The whole team guided her in practice for an hour and twenty minutes, and then retouched everything.

Five minutes before their departure, Roz cleared her throat and the entire room stopped.

"It is time for the mask."

The girl in black and the one with the asymmetric haircut scurried out of the room, while the woman with the perfect face clapped her hands together and the bald man smiled.

Mina's stomach sank. The mask. She would wear it until midnight, at which point she would remove it and reveal to Cyrano their sham of a queen. Roz and her team could make her look the part all they wanted, but she would never truly be the stuff of queens.

The two women came back into the room, carefully carrying what looked like a small sun.

It was Mina's mask.

Fitting snugly around the top half of her head, it was made out of soft yellow-gold fabric, with long beams jutting out from it in a haloed crown of rays. It wasn't a mask that was about disguising the Queen until the big moment as much as it was a mask about identifying where to look when the time came.

It gave off its own light, for goodness' sake.

It was a spectacular creation.

Between the dress and the mask, no one would be able to take their eyes off her.

Words rose up and got trapped in her throat.

Between the gown and the mask, she would be the center of attention—Roz's grand finale.

It was all too much.

The stylist carefully placed the mask over her head, securing the latch that would hold it in place until she pressed the release button.

As she did so, the woman with the perfect face hissed, "Careful with my masterpiece."

The bald man hurried over to adjust individual curls once the mask was in place, and then stepped back with a smile.

Mina looked once more into the mirror.

The beautiful creature that stared back was made of living, breathing gold—exuding class and style despite the shine.

Tonight, the sun would set on Mina the scholar and rise on Mina the Queen.

CHAPTER FOUR

RATHER THAN CHECK the alert when it buzzed through on his phone, Zayn checked his watch.

There was still an hour and a half until the start of the ball, and the car that would drive him was not due to arrive for an hour.

He could be getting ready. The timing was not unreasonable. In fact, his assistant had been anxiously glancing at the wall clock for at least twenty minutes.

Zayn ignored both of those observations. He was determined to finish reviewing the pair of trade agreements in front of him before he allowed Mina and her ball any more space in his mind. She had been a constant presence in it over the past week and a half, despite the fact that Zayn had expended actual time and energy to ensure that she would not be in his presence.

His wife.

He would not spend his time lost in thought about his wife.

Not when there was work to be done. He refused. He was not his father, who had not been above putting off his royal responsibilities to spend time with his wife.

Zayn would not be that man. Nothing came before Cyrano. His time of being irresponsibly carefree and open had ended the day his father had been shot. As King, he had no time for brown-skinned women with moss-colored eyes who lingered in his thoughts.

He refused to waste any time on leisurely preparing his attire, like some kind of old-fashioned dandy. He might have been born into royalty, but his father had instilled in him a sense of proportion.

He turned his attention back to the agreements, his will an iron wall around his mind, defending it from the obsessive onslaught of green eyes and wayward thoughts.

Forty minutes later he was nearly two-thirds of the way through the second agreement when his phone vibrated again. Once again, he ignored it.

"Your Majesty."

Frowning, he turned his attention to his assistant. "Yes?" he asked tersely.

"I think you should see this." The man held up his phone, a slight tremor in his arm.

The headline read: *All Hail Queen Midas!* Below it was a full-body picture of Mina who, unveiled in her ball attire, revealed a body that indeed looked sculpted from gold.

She had even more curves than he'd imagined. Heels lengthened her impossibly long legs, which were clearly outlined for the first time since he'd seen them by garments that actually fit. She held her shoulders straight, her posture holding the same determination he'd witnessed her summoning for him, and the effect only enhanced her high-breasted glory.

Her mask was immense, its rays stretching out to create an invisible bubble between her and anyone who might get too close to her radiant form.

She wasn't merely gorgeous.

She was the force of gravity at the center of the universe.

And she was walking the red carpet early.

Without him.

He pulled out his phone at the same time as its buzzing began in earnest. Alert after alert—curated courtesy of the fact that he'd set a news alert to monitor mentions of the Queen—popped up on his screen.

As images of her loaded, blood rushed in his ears, and he acknowledged to himself that he was not going to finish the trade agreements.

Pushing his chair away from his desk, he stood and stepped around the heavy furniture.

His assistant, still scrolling through images

himself, started at the King's sudden movement, but quickly followed as Zayn strode out of his office.

As they walked, Zayn instructed him to have his closet man prepare his clothes and his barber meet him in his parlor.

It was time to get ready for the ball.

His clothing arrived in his room at the same time as he did and he dressed quickly, appreciating the ease of perfect tailoring. One never had to worry how one looked when one's clothes were made for one's body.

Commissioned for the event, the tuxedo was entirely black, made from thick Chinese silk. Each element of his attire, from the jacket to the butter-smooth button-down shirt, was perfectly coordinated and fitted to his body alone. Nothing about anything he wore spoke of it being a costume, and yet when he placed the midnight domino mask on his face there was no mistaking him for anything other than the King of the night himself.

The unforgiving black of the silk absorbed all light that touched it, calling to mind a dark moonless night in the dead of winter.

How convenient that Mina was the sun personified.

Ten minutes later he was in his car, on his way.

His driver pulled up and cameras flashed as he stepped out onto the red carpet.

His arrival had disrupted the flow of other prominent citizens, but he didn't slow for photos, reaching the entrance stairs quickly and taking them two at a time.

The lobby of the grand theater had been transformed, though he had little attention for its grandeur as he cut through the parting crowd.

Inside, all of the seats had been removed and temporary flooring installed, creating the impression of walking upon a vast expanse of space. In fact the entire lower half of the large room had become the night sky, brought indoors. Taking advantage of the theater's classic gilded ceilings, the upper half of the room was an homage to daylight. Balconies had become starbursts and sunbeams. And the stage was the meeting of day and night—a twilight alcove, romantically furnished, clearly the resting place for the stars of the evening: the King and the Queen.

But she was not there.

Instead, she stood across the room, engrossed in conversation with the French ambassador.

Zayn's brow crinkled in irritation. The ambassador was a lecherous middle-aged man who had no business standing so close to the Queen of Cyrano—especially not with that appreciative light in his eyes.

Not that he could blame him.

She was divine. And she was the true meaning of the word "radiant" as a petite woman dressed all in black led her along the outer edge of the ballroom.

Moustafa and d'Tierrza followed at a close distance behind them.

The theater was crowded, with barely enough room to move around. Even this early in the evening elegantly costumed couples spun around the dance floor in the center of the room, while other partygoers milled about anywhere there was room. Wait staff carrying trays laden with champagne flutes and hors d'oeuvres wove through the crowd, handing out their wares.

For a moment, Zayn simply watched her.

Awareness of his presence, however, soon spread through the crowd, bringing a hush to the group despite the fact that the music continued.

Slowly the people parted, opening a pathway between Mina and himself. She did not notice—perhaps because she had moved on from the French ambassador and was now involved in what looked like an intense conversation with the Minister of Agriculture.

Zayn approached her without her knowing, observing as he neared that the lines of her back, revealed and accentuated as they were by her astonishing gown, were obviously the shared creation of heaven and hell.

Her spine was a graceful indentation that slid and flowed between her slim shoulder blades, drawing his gaze to the generous swell of her hips. If there was ever a reason to burn all the trousers in the country, it would be because Mina had once used them to commit the sacrilege of hiding her glorious backside.

The dress did sinful things to her legs, too. Seeing her clothed in garments that actually fit, he could now see that her legs were the true source of her above average height. And tonight she was even taller than usual—a tall golden bouquet of curves and curls.

And there was another surprise.

Freed from the severe braid, her hair was riotous—sensual, soft, and mesmerizing. He fought the urge to thrust his hand into the vibrant cloud of her hair, palm the back of her hand, and bend her face back towards his. Instead, he curled his fingers around the soft exposed flesh of her upper arm, running his thumb along the buttery-soft smoothness of her skin.

Up close, the thin film of her dress seemed so viscerally alive it was as if he felt it shiver along with the rest of her body at his touch. His senses zeroed in on her further, taking in the flush beneath the glow that hadn't been there moments before.

The music still continued, but all eyes in the room were on the King and his unknown Queen.

She turned slowly, forcing him to release her arm.

His eyes burned over her body like a grassland fire as she rotated, taking in the curve of her hips and indentation of her waist.

The front of the dress was even more of a revelation.

A full-grown woman had been hiding beneath all that oversized clothing.

He felt her with his gaze as he raked it upwards, spending extra time on her proud breasts before finally letting it make its way up to meet the wide-stretched green eyes behind the mask—eyes that had haunted him since the moment he'd seen them in the chapel.

Her breath caught, but she held her composure, giving a small vertical curtsy and murmuring, "Your Majesty." Her voice was cool, but as taut as the rest of her body.

He inclined his head, addressing her with the same cool tone. "Your Majesty."

Mina opened her mouth to speak again and Zayn felt his pulse quicken, waiting for what she would say, but the petite woman in black had stepped from behind her, holding a milky stone circlet out to him.

Her voice cracked out like a dry whip. "You're late, Your Majesty. Put this on."

Zayn's spine straightened at the familiar rasp, his hand automatically reaching out to accept the offering—obedience to this particular individual had been drilled into him since childhood.

"Roz." He inclined his head to her respectfully, before looking at what he held. It was a black circlet inlaid with moonstone. He put it on without comment.

Roz had been his royal etiquette instructor throughout his childhood. Now she was the most sought-after event-planner in the kingdom. She was also his godmother.

A number of things about the evening made abrupt sense.

"Please join us in making the rounds, Your Majesty," Roz said.

Beside her, Mina stiffened.

Roz's request had been more order than invitation, but she was one of the few people the King still deferred to.

"It would be my honor, Roz."

He reached an arm out to the older woman, but she gave a small shake of her head. Telling himself he was doing as he was told because it was Roz, rather than because he wanted to get his hands on the silk that was Mina, he smoothly took her arm in his.

As their skin touched her scent rose up and wrapped around him—fresh and floral, with just a hint of something wicked. He closed his eyes, resisting the urge to bend his head to her neck and breathe deep.

Her flush deepened and he felt the heat of it emanating from her body. Rather than stop himself, he leaned in a fraction of an inch closer to her and breathed in her heat and her scent. Her eyes widened into mossy pools beneath her mask and her mouth opened slightly in surprise, her body frozen by his gaze.

His impact on her was obvious. The power and thrill that came with it, however, was unexpected. He was used to power. He was the King, with power over millions of souls. And yet this power... He had a feeling his power to affect this woman was somehow singular.

Roz cleared her throat loudly, saying, "If we may...?" And the moment evaporated.

Like good little soldiers, he and Mina turned at attention, in unison, but out of the corner of his eye he could see that wherever there was skin visible Mina had blushed a deep red.

Fixing him with a long stare, Roz led their trio toward another diplomat—this one from the United Kingdom.

A distinguished older man, Charles William Henry was a minor aristocrat in his home country. As its official ambassador to Cyrano, however, he held a high enough status to warrant a personal greeting from the King and Queen— Zayn credited that fact with his seeking of the position in the first place.

"Your Majesty…" The man oozed over Mina's hand with an enthusiasm that grated on Zayn's ears. "It is truly a pleasure to finally make your acquaintance. I must say it was worth the wait, however. You are more radiant than the sun. Apollo must bow when you enter a room."

Zayn didn't know which was more grating on his nerves: the man's abysmal poetry or the way he extended every syllable in his exaggerated posh accent.

Below her mask, however, Mina smiled. It was the first true smile Zayn had ever seen her wear, and it spread across the lower portion of her face, showing too many teeth for a proper queen's smile, but all the more bright and breathtaking for it. It cut through him as if he were a storm cloud and she a literal ray of sunshine.

Only the fact that it had been a rain of asinine compliments that had somehow managed to make her glow kept him from falling under the spell of the smile himself.

"You are too kind, sir. I understand your family owns property in the South of England? I have always heard the country there is lovely."

Both men started when she spoke. Her English was clear and understandable, if slightly North-American-accented, and Zayn found himself perversely pleased that, wherever she had learned the language, it had not been Britain.

"You speak English, Your Majesty!" the ambassador exclaimed. "When I learned you were native to Cyrano, I did not expect it—most citizens don't, as you know," he said, insulting their country with mock abashment. "Indeed, Your Majesty, I *am* from the south of England. Thank you for noticing. And, yes, there is nothing quite like it. It would be my honor to host you there. I am certain I could give you a proper English time."

A muscle in the back of Zayn's neck twitched as the man's words grew bolder with each passing moment. Establishing a bond between the two kingdoms had been one of Zayn's many coups. Great Britain was a global power. The fact that it would acknowledge Cyrano as anything more than a Mediterranean backwater had been unprecedented.

However, now, as the ambassador undressed the Queen with his eyes, his voice dripping with suggestion, Zayn found himself wondering how necessary that diplomatic relationship really was.

Resisting the urge to put the question to the test, Zayn simply put himself between the other man and the Queen, responding for her, his voice as soft as velvet as it wrapped around the English words.

"Of course there will be tours in the future. However, I plan to keep my new bride to myself for as long as possible. Newlyweds—I'm sure you understand."

He guided Mina away from the man with Roz following.

"Very subtle and diplomatic, Zayn," she observed.

The humor in Roz's voice eased the tension in his neck as if he were slipping into well-worn leather boot, gently reminding him that he was acting like a fool.

Rather than respond to that, though, he said, "I assume you're behind Mina's transformation?"

"Well, hello to you too, Your Royal Majesty."

Mina's voice matched Roz's for dryness. Zayn shuddered to think what else she might have picked up from her time with the older woman.

"You were late," Roz observed.

They were ganging up on him.

Zayn smiled, "And I thought you were early."

Again, Roz snorted. "A queen is never early."

She started to guide their group forward again—Zayn imagined to make more introductions. But he found he did not care to continue the rounds, filing away the name of each and every single man who stared overlong at the Queen, when he could have the golden star of the night all to himself.

Roz pointed them toward a cluster of popular musicians, but Zayn shook his head. "The Queen is wilting." He nodded toward Mina who, if anything, glowed with her own inner light.

"I'm fine, thank you," she said, irritation threading through her voice.

He shook his head distinctly, negating her statement. "You are a dimming sun. It's time for you to set. You can't be used to standing in heels for so long."

Mina's mouth dropped into the O of outrage he was so familiar with and he smiled. Roz lifted her eyebrow at being crossed, but gave a short nod, watching their interaction closely. She could add it to the list of transgressions he was sure he would hear about from her later.

Leaving her to act as hostess, he led Mina to the stage and helped her into the seat that had clearly been designed for her dress. She didn't sit, exactly, as much as recline regally. A subtle golden spotlight beamed down on her where she rested, maintaining her haloed image even as a very human sigh escaped her.

At her side, of the same height as her unique

chair, was a dark, high-backed throne, obviously intended for him. She would look like a celestial sphinx stretched out next to a dark midnight king. Even sitting, the royal couple would remain the center of attention—and conversation—for the night.

Roz had considered every detail.

Rather than simply letting the old devil have her way, though, he remained standing. Mina stared up at him, her eyes glowing especially green in the light, and he had to fight the urge to dive into their mossy depths. This close, he was caught in the web of her scent and temperature, mesmerized by the thin silk of her dress, which seemed to reveal more and more to delight his eyes the longer he was near her.

He sucked in a deep breath.

The effect she was having on him was a manufactured thing, created by Roz, and yet knowing that did nothing to dampen it.

Pulling his attention away from her, he lifted his hand in a signal for refreshments.

In an instant a quintet of servers arrived, their heavy platters laden, offering each option on the floor.

He reached for two flutes of champagne and offered her the first selection. Taking the glass, she thanked him before choosing a small cracker dressed with some kind of cheese and slivers of tomato and basil from one of the trays. She ate delicately, for all that her morsel disappeared in one bite, and he watched her do it, arrested by the series of movements in her eating, from the parting of her full lips to the contraction of her throat muscles as she swallowed.

He shook his head lightly. He needed to get away from her. He would leave immediately after the unmasking. Until then, he would remain in the place Roz had clearly assigned him, as a king on full display.

"Roz outdid herself tonight," he commented.

"She did." Her words were clipped and close.

He felt irritation rising in his blood. She was wary. *Of him.*

"Admirable of you to admit it," he said dryly.

Instead of rising to his bait, Mina smiled. "It would have been a disaster without Roz." She waved her hand toward the room, adding, "Instead, it's the sun and the moon."

"She knows how to throw a party," he agreed.

This time Mina laughed, and the honest clarity of the sound went straight into his blood, as energizing as it was agitating.

"That's quite the understatement," she said, when she could speak.

The corners of his own lips lifted of their own accord, and behind her mask her eyes widened.

His chest heated with pure male satisfaction. He wasn't the only one caught up in Roz's mirage.

With a nod, he said, "The woman is a force of nature."

As if sensing their conversation, Roz appeared on the stage, accompanied by a tall, slender older woman in an elegant blue gown and a peacock feather mask.

Zayn rose and gave the woman a bow. "Aunt Seraphina."

The woman nodded to him with a smile, "It's supposed to be a mystery, Your Majesty."

"My apologies. You look lovely."

Seraphina d'Tierrza, his maternal aunt, shook her head with a mild reprimand. "Flattering an old woman when you have your beautiful Queen beside you?"

Her voice was as warm and as gently teasing as it had been when he was a little boy, caught climbing trees with her daughter.

Zayn offered Mina a hand, their fingers exchanging a mild electric shock upon contact, and when she stood her scent once again wrapped around him, capturing his complete attention, even if for only a moment.

Mina reached a hand out to Seraphina. "It's so wonderful to finally meet you. Your daughter has been heaven-sent."

Her voice followed the model of her scent, its warm tones enveloping him in her spell.

"I'm glad you think so, Your Majesty. Not everyone has the sense to appreciate her as you do. We are very proud of her being a member of your guard."

"More than that." Mina smiled. "She is a friend."

His aunt beamed beneath the new young Queen's words and Zayn frowned.

"You are truly the gem my Helene claimed you to be." His aunt's voice sparkled.

Surely his aunt—the sister of a queen herself, and the nation's only remaining duchess—could see how unsuitable Mina was for her new role. Yet here she was, extending a warm familial welcome to the cuckoo in the nest.

He'd always thought of his aunt among the least sentimental of the bunch. Of course, Mina *had* just complimented her child. Every mother had a weak spot when it came to flattery of her children.

Roz led Seraphina away after a few more pleasantries, only to return with someone new. The woman was obviously determined they circulate, even if she had to bring people to them. The observation brought with it a mischievous spark he hadn't felt since he and his cousin's days of scheming to evade Roz "the dragon lady" and her plans.

As it had then, Zayn's mind bent itself to the creative task as Roz led away her latest guest to exchange him for another.

Turning to Mina, he smiled, drawing her into the game that had only ever belonged to him and his cousin. "We're going to dance," he said.

Unexpectedly, Mina shook her head in a fast and firm negative.

"You can't tell me you are enjoying this introduction train?" he asked imperiously.

Mina swallowed, but she held her ground with another slight shake of the head.

Out of the corner of his eye he saw Roz making her way through the crowd with the Dowager Countess of Redcliff. Their progress was slow, as the one-hundred-and-four-year-old Countess moved rather...deliberately.

"You must," he commanded, holding out his hand to assist her.

If she did not take his hand it would be in the news tomorrow. He wondered if she'd realized that yet.

Fortunately, she did not put it to the test, taking his hand with a sigh.

"We're not going to dance," she insisted.

And then he understood. And, like the spark that had had him leading her to the floor, a boyish thrill shot through his veins.

"You can't dance."

It wasn't a question.

She blushed, but gave a sharp nod.

He laughed. "Of course you can't."

Mina winced, but his grin only grew.

"Don't worry, Mina mine. I am an excellent lead."

"You're something, all right," she muttered.

He led her on, riding high on the strange cocktail of youthful excitement and lust stirring in his blood. They passed Roz and the Dowager Countess as they made their way to the floor. Roz's eyes narrowed at the King, and their glances were exchanged in the knowledge that she knew exactly what he was up to.

His grin stretched wider, and even the indomitable Roz was affected, the firm lines of her glare softening.

But softening was not the same as disappearing altogether.

Catching Zayn's arm in her bony talon as they passed, Roz hissed, "The unmasking will happen at the end of your dance! You'll have to take the mask off for her—there's a clasp in the back."

Then she let them go.

Zayn led Mina to the dance floor, a pathway clearing before them. Other dancers left the floor as they approached the center, a warm spotlight finding them as they came to a stop, facing each other.

He wasn't sure whether it was due to the rush

of success in dodging Roz, or simply the primal effect of Mina's radiant glow in the spotlight, but although they were surrounded, the rest of the room slowly disappeared as he looked at her.

Reaching out his arms, he took her by the waist and pulled her body flush against his. As tall as she was in the heels and the mask, her head still came only to his shoulder, allowing him to rest his cheek on the smooth front of her mask, his own expression shielded by the emanating rays.

Her dress was a warm second skin beneath his palm and her lush curves pressed against the hard planes of his own body. Heat and blood rushed to his core as if this were the first time he'd ever drawn a woman close on a dance floor.

Her palm came to rest softly at his shoulder while he stretched their arms out, hands gently clasped. She sucked in a breath, her breasts brushing against his chest in the process, the sensation stealing his own breath.

The orchestra struck up his favorite waltz.

He had no idea who the performers were, but they knew his favorite waltz.

It was good to be King.

Zayn drew her into the dance, and for first time since he'd met her she gracefully followed his lead.

The floor had cleared completely by this point, and he took advantage of the space to set them a double-time pace, leaving her breathless and clinging to him. Smile wide, she seemed too focused on holding him to be nervous. Scientist that she was, she gave in to the momentum of their bodies, allowing her hips to press into his naturally, reminding him exactly why this dance had been banned during his country's more conservative historical eras.

So focused was his mind on the press and heat of her that it took him some time to realize that the joyful notes weaving their way into the music were the sound of her laughter. Bubbling around them, it wove its way into his blood like the finest champagne, silky and reserved for an exchange of goods that cost far more than money.

He slowed down as the familiar chords came to their conclusion until they stood together in the large warm spotlight, chests pressed close and lifting in unison, eyes locked on each other.

Conversation in the room fell silent.

As if compelled, she lifted her hands to the sides of his face. Zayn closed his eyes as her fingertips trailed through his hair, seeking and finding the thin leather straps that held his domino mask in place. He felt a small surge of power as her eyes widened when she removed the mask. She would never be able to hide her reaction to him. Somehow he knew that.

He pulled the mask from her hand and dropped

it to the ground without a glance, then drew the
pads of her fingertips to his mouth, to place small
kisses on each one. Then he drew her closer to
reach his hands around her neck and find the
clasp at the back of her mask.

He pressed the release and the mask unlocked.

With two hands, he lifted it from her head
slowly. Two servers appeared at his side to carefully carry the solid gold creation away.

Bright curls exploded around Mina's head, re-
placing the mask to bathe and halo her face in
light.

Her face was even more of a masterpiece than
the mask. Gold flakes sparkled in the emerald of
her irises, and the creamy golden brown of her
skin glowed in the light. She was all sparkling
eyes and slightly parted plush lips, and there was
nothing for him to do but thrust his fingers into
her hair, cup the back of her skull where it met
her neck, and possess her.

Her breath caught as their lips met, etching the
moment into memory through all of his senses—
taste, touch, sight, scent, and sound. Her lips were
velvet-soft and plump as she leaned into him, returning the kiss, as lost as he was to the current
sweeping over them.

The crowd erupted into cheers, abruptly grind-
ing the madness to a halt—he was the King and
this display was unseemly—and yet he still broke

the kiss gently, unable to rip himself away from her despite his horror at what he had just done.

Her eyes fluttered open, clouded still with the haze of their kiss, and, fighting the urge to pull her back to him, he acknowledged that forgetting decorum seemed to be one of the results of proximity to Mina.

Slowly, but with a flourish, he spun her out to his side and raised her arm, the smooth flow of his movements smoothing over his breach of etiquette and giving him some distance from its cause at the same time.

Another cheer rang out from the crowd. Cyrano loved its new Queen. Now Zayn just had to figure out what to do about it.

CHAPTER FIVE

A MASSIVE POUNDING shook Mina from a heavy sleep and what she was sure had been a pleasant dream. Warm lethargy lingered in her body and almost had her rolling over to try to find it again.

Unfortunately, the pounding continued.

Groaning, she sat up—only to realize that not all the noise was coming from *outside* her head.

And here, she'd always heard that fine champagne didn't have consequences…

Lifting the weighted comforter in order to get up, she was startled to realize she wore only the thin strip of cloth that the styling team all seemed to agree was underwear.

To her horror, the golden dress lay in a puddle on the floor beside the bed, alongside the heels that had had her feet aching by the end of the night. She realized she had no idea what had become of her mask.

The sheets were smooth and slick where they touched her bare skin, which should have been a soothing counter to the pounding in her head, but as she typically slept in an oversized T-shirt rather than *au naturel*, the sensation only served to accentuate the sense of unfamiliarity.

Once covered, she answered her suite door.

Moustafa and d'Tierrza stood on the other side, the latter grinning like a fool.

"Good morning, sunshine! You've been summoned."

Her brow crinkling, Mina's voice was a dry croak. "Summoned?"

D'Tierrza rolled her eyes. "His Royal Majesty has commanded your presence at breakfast."

Mina frowned. Not once in the time since she'd been at the palace had Zayn requested her presence for a meal. Of course, that had been before he had kissed her in front of the entire country. ·

The memory of it flooded her senses as she stood in the doorway.

He'd kissed her on the dance floor, in view of everyone in attendance, and then there had been too many toasts to count, as if they were celebrating the dawn of a new year, rather than a new queen.

Mina groaned and squeezed her eyes shut. Now, at least to the rest of the world, their marriage was very real.

Dressing quickly, she met her guards at the

door, flashing her best determined smile and saying, "Lead the way."

The two guards led Mina through a new series of twisting hallways and corridors until they came to yet another set of high wooden doors.

Moustafa and d'Tierrza pressed them open for her and Mina walked in, her head high. She would face the King this morning with dignity—even if she had no idea how you faced someone you had kissed.

The King sat at the end of a long table, face hidden behind his newspaper. It occurred to Mina that the length of the dining table and hall seemed particularly excessive when one was slowly approaching one's mercurial husband who had kissed one the night before.

A staff member in crisply starched attire rushed forward to pull out her chair as she neared, and the King finally lowered his paper.

As always, his beauty struck Mina like a physical blow. In the fresh morning light the darkness of his hair and the deep violet of his eyes were so pure she could drown in them. As usual, he wore all black. This morning his clothing consisted of a perfectly tailored black button-up shirt with a sheen to it, and trim black pants that appeared to flow with the line of his leg like water.

The table was set with breakfast for two, and it

crossed Mina's mind that her presence had been assumed. Summoned, indeed...

The King cleared his throat as the breakfast server pushed her chair in for her, and his brows came together in a frown as he took in her appearance.

"They're calling it a love match," he said.

"Excuse me?" she choked out.

"The nation's media outlets are quite abuzz about it this morning. They say I fell madly in love with a commoner. The story is currently the most trending topic online in Cyrano."

Mina's stomach twisted. "Should we correct them?"

At the King's decisive shake of his head she felt some of the tension ease in her. She didn't know what that reaction said about her integrity, but the thought of clarifying the nature of their relationship for the public was more than she could bear.

"It serves no purpose. However, I prefer that my personal life not be the nation's most trending topic. Therefore, we're going to the summer palace, in order to give the public time to find something else to fixate upon."

"We are?"

"We'll leave by the end of the day. The Champions League finals begin in three days. That should be enough distraction to supersede any gossip about us. We will be gone for five days, as we must be here in attendance for the Ambassadors' Dinner on the fifteenth. Are you going to eat or simply stare at your plate?"

"Yes..." Mina said, reaching to serve herself from the platters of fruit and pastries and fluffy golden eggs laid out in front of her—though she wasn't sure she was hungry, and this was the first she was hearing about the Ambassadors' Dinner. Her secretary probably thought she had enough to deal with before then.

"We will leave here at five p.m. We'll have a late meal at the summer palace, and then enjoy the island. The Ambassadors' Dinner is one of the less glamorous royal engagements. Returning for that should keep any mention of us to the government pages, rather than the front page of the culture section."

He indicated the paper he'd set aside earlier, and Mina noticed the picture for the first time.

It was her and Zayn, their bodies molded to one another, lips pressed close—the very picture of a man and woman in love, or at the very least in lust.

Her cheeks heated, flushing beet-red through the brown of her skin.

The passion between the couple in the photo was undeniable, and yet none of it was real. Her husband was a stranger who could barely stand the sight of her. He certainly didn't harbor any passion for her.

Her stomach churned again, threatening to upend the few bites of breakfast she had managed to swallow.

The King appeared indifferent, as if being discussed in the newspapers and photographed in such a personal embrace was a common occurrence for him. Though, come to think of it, it probably was. He had likely been photographed kissing women more times than he could count— whereas she could say with certainty that she had never been photographed anywhere so near *in flagrante delicto* as this.

It was easy to be certain when you had only ever had one kiss in your whole life. And now hers had been immortalized on the front page of the "Arts & Culture" section of the *Cyranese Times*.

She wondered if this was what her father had had in mind when he'd given her away to the King. He'd certainly been vigilant in protecting her chastity.

"Boys? Sss! No boys! You have no time for boys. Not when you must work. Work hard, my Princess, for the good of Cyrano."

She hated it that what had seemed like memories of normal fatherly protectiveness had come to take on such a cynical nature now. And it wasn't just her memories. It was her entire life.

She had been so proud of her accomplishments. It hadn't been easy to become the youngest female scientist ever nominated for the King's council. But the years of sacrifice, the endurance, the at times cruel reshaping of herself—now she couldn't figure out exactly why she had done any of it.

She had thought it was because it was the one thing she had left of her father—the final living ember of a love that she had thought as transparent as it had been absolute. But she had been wrong—so wrong. All of it had been done so that rather than being a private miracle, her first kiss could be the stuff of headlines.

The thought was like a rock in her stomach.

She ate without noticing flavor or texture, her mind churning over the photo and the kiss. It seemed Zayn wasn't going to mention it at all. Was a front-page kiss so commonplace to him that it didn't bear remark?

Looking at him surreptitiously out of the corner of her eye, she imagined that, once again, the answer was yes. A kiss wouldn't mean much to a man who looked like him—let alone one who had grown up as the heir to the throne and then become King. She imagined women had been throwing themselves at him since long before it had been allowed according to the Cyranese age of consent laws.

He ate deliberately, clearly feeling no need to fill the silence that stretched between them. In the absence of conversation, the sounds of their eating filled the quiet morning—however, instead of feeling awkward, the experience of eating breakfast with the King was somehow more intimate for its lack of forced chatter.

Mina was reminded of the mornings of her childhood, the details of individual days blurring together to emphasize what had been commonplace: her mother and father moving in sync through the steps of their morning routine with the practiced familiarity of a long marriage.

The memory was a painful twist in her chest. The silence of those mornings had been companionable, unlike the quiet that enveloped her and the King now, and yet the comparison lingered in her mind just the same.

She and the King shared no loving glances, and their eyes were not full of the previous night's memories and plans for the day ahead. Neither of them reached toward the other with small caresses or touch points. And yet they were still a man and a woman—husband and wife—sharing a meal. She certainly hadn't shared the experience with any other men in her life.

The realization was both revealing and sad. It

was becoming more and more clear to her that she should have gotten out more. She hadn't needed to sow her wild oats, but it wouldn't have hurt her or derailed her career to go on a date once in her life. And it would have certainly gone a long way toward her not being the kind of woman so starved for companionship that she was finding it in a stilted meal with a stranger.

"Where is the summer palace?" she asked, both to break the silence and to stem the internal tide of self-recrimination.

Turning the full power of his attention to her, the King replied, "Cantorini Island."

She started. She'd heard the name of the famous private island, but had had no idea it was tied to the royal family. "I've heard it's beautiful there."

The King smiled, his features softening in the process, making him look almost boyish. "It is. It's private, of course, and remote. The only structures on the island are associated with the summer palace compound. It's a wonderful escape from the constant observation of the capital."

Between his smile and the open warmth of his tone, Mina's heart stuttered. He had no idea how dangerous he was.

"There are supposed to be multiple species endemic to the island," she said, inwardly cringing at this offering to the conversation as soon as it was out.

But the King's smile grew. "That's right. Most of the island is vegetated, and it provides excellent habitat for a number of native species. We occasionally allow groups of biologists and students access, for observation and data collection."

The corners of Mina's lips lifted in response. "That's right! I considered applying for the trip between my junior and sophomore years of college, but I was selected for a fellowship in the Galapagos instead."

"Well, as you have the opportunity to visit now, it appears you made the right choice at the time."

The stiff response hung between them, effectively cooling the warmth that had grown.

"Yes. Well…" Mina searched for a smooth exit but, finding none, settled on, "I have some coordinating to do in order to be ready to leave this afternoon, so…"

Telling herself that the fact that the King looked mildly relieved at her words stung only a little bit, Mina rose as he said, "Yes, of course. Five o'clock, then."

Mina nodded, excusing herself from the long dining room and letting out a sigh only after shutting the door behind her.

Moustafa and d'Tierrza stood to attention on either side of the door. Sensing them, Mina took a breath and straightened her shoulders. She never would have guessed it could happen, but she was actually coming to find comfort in the constancy of their presence.

With a half-smile, she said, "Well, ladies, it looks like we're going to the summer palace."

D'Tierrza started, before quickly catching Moustafa's eye.

Mina was immediately uneasy. "What?"

Moustafa opened her mouth to say something, only to close it again. On her second try, she got out, "Guards are not allowed at the summer palace."

Mina's eyebrows came together. "That doesn't make any sense."

D'Tierrza took over. "The summer palace is a retreat for the royal family—a place for them to go to feel normal. The staff there live in residence year-round, are heavily vetted, and are all military trained. With them around, members of the royal family can be free to go about their day safely, without guards."

"But that means it will be just the two of us…"

Moustafa winced at Mina's forlorn tone.

D'Tierrza let out a bark of laughter and began to lead them back towards the Queen's Wing. "You'll love Cantorini. Just make sure to have the staff pack some books…" D'Tierrza narrowed her eyes at her Queen "…and a swimsuit."

Nine hours later a chauffeur opened the back door of a sleek black SUV and Mina got in, her bags long-ago stowed and packed by someone else, filled with mysterious clothing items selected by her staff. She imagined there was a swimsuit somewhere in there…

The thought brought a smile to her face—which was more than could be said for the King, who had followed her into the car before the chauffeur shut the door behind him.

Though he'd said no more than a few words to her in greeting, his presence had dominated her senses from the moment they'd met outside the palace at one of the many private entrances.

Like her, he wore the same clothes he had at breakfast. Unlike her, he remained as flawlessly put together as he had been that morning.

As spacious as the vehicle they were enclosed in was, his fragrance still enveloped her, throwing her back to the sensation of being wrapped up in him, his lips pressed against hers.

Mina's breath caught as she tamped down the memory. That was most certainly not the thing to think about while traveling alone and in close quarters with the King.

"Was the rest of your day productive?" she asked, hoping shop talk would do the job of breaking the tension between them.

Swinging his gaze lazily to capture hers, he

let his eyes pin her against the seat. Her breath caught. His nostrils flared slightly and she felt herself lean forward, drawn toward him despite the danger obvious in his regard.

A spark lit in his stare at her movement, the corner of his mouth lifting slightly, and she realized he knew the effect he had on her. Something wild and indignant in her demanded she break free of the hold, but he was too strong.

His words were drawn out, slow and languid in a way she'd never heard him speak before, when he asked, "Do you really care how my day went?"

And although her body shivered at all the unspoken things in his voice that showed what he thought she really cared about, Mina found herself surprised by the truth in her words when she replied, a tad breathlessly, "Yes."

Something in her reply took him aback, though she didn't know if it was the honesty that had surprised her, or the unspoken invitation to talk about statecraft itself.

He shrugged and sat back, snapping the tautness between them as he traded a bit of languid grace for upright alertness. Mina found herself regretting the loss.

"I secured two new international trade agreements, resisted a foreign power's overreach into Cyranese affairs, and set the stage for establishing an official diplomatic relationship with the Kingdom of Montenegro."

Mina's breath caught in her throat. The fact that he had answered—and not facetiously—felt somehow more important than it probably was. But it was what he'd said, the casual mention of allegiances and world politics, which shook her to the core. He was the King. His days were comprised of the stuff of nations.

And what were *her* days comprised of? Royal summonses and waiting for others to coordinate her luggage. Falling softly back against the seat, she mourned the loss of her old identity once more.

Queen Amina's days were idled away. Dr. Mina Aldaba's days had been spent in research and study, her mind applied to the most pressing concerns of modern science.

But she had asked the King a question, and she was being rude in dwelling on herself. "That sounds like a very productive day," she said.

He smirked at her. "Where did I lose you? Trade agreements?"

Mina frowned. "Of course not. I understand how important advantageous trade agreements are for a small nation like ours."

His smirk blossomed into a real smile, and Mina realized he'd deliberately worked a rise out of her. Her own lips stretched wide, unconsciously imitating his light expression, and as they did so his face changed, as if he were suddenly transfixed.

How long they would have stayed that way, staring at one another, Mina had no idea, but fortunately the car came to a stop, breaking the moment.

Seconds later the door opened and the chauffeur offered her a hand. Stepping out onto Tarmac, Mina deduced that they must be taking the small plane that waited about six meters away, its rounded door open, a stairway lowered.

Attendants ushered them quickly to the plane. On board, the King checked the safety equipment before showing Mina the amenities. About halfway through the mini-tour, Mina realized the plane was his private plane, and that he loved it.

"The flight is short—just forty-five minutes in the air—but it's the safest way to get to the island at this time of year."

His posture had lost some its characteristic rigidity since they'd boarded the plane, and his voice had taken on a note of youthful excitement that hinted at the kind of man he might have been before his father's death.

The idea filled Mina with the strangest urge to have known him then—before he became King. She didn't know where it came from, but she couldn't shake the sensation that he must have been different—lighter, more joyful.

"I've never taken such a short flight," she said, although the scientist in her was frowning somewhat at the impact this small flight might have on a delicate eco-system like Cantorini's.

Reading her mind, the King said, "The benefit of a plane this size is that we've been able to retrofit it to run on completely renewable energy. In fact, the entire summer palace was updated six years ago, to achieve a net zero impact on the island. The technology isn't scalable for all of Cyrano yet, but at this point it's just a matter of time."

She was impressed. While wealth like the royal family's made such experimentation infinitely more possible, not many who had the capacity also had the will.

"That's wonderful. Your parents must have had excellent forethought to do that. So when do we take off?" she asked.

But the King shook his head. "It was my idea. I pestered my father until he was willing to do anything to shut me up."

His eyes lit with the memory, his smile turning into a downright grin, and Mina was enchanted. "It must've cost a fortune," she said.

His grin stretched. "It did. Well worth it to

know the future of the island is safer, though. I've always loved going there."

"I can imagine. A place to run around like a normal child... That had to be precious to you."

His face softened as he nodded. "It was. It can be a challenge to be a prince and a child at the same time."

Her heart reached out to that boy with the pressure of a nation on his shoulders. Her own childhood had been bright and free, even though she now knew that her father had arranged for her to be a queen before it had even begun. Her dreams and his encouragement had pushed her to achieve, but for all the striving she'd still been a normal girl. Her parents had ensured that.

"I'm glad you had a place to escape."

He turned to face her at her words, searching her face for something, and even though she didn't know how she knew, she could sense it was genuineness. Her heart broke for him. He was adored and idolized by an entire nation, and yet starving for everyday acts of compassion.

She had the feeling he didn't have many people he could talk to.

"Me too," he said. "I was fortunate that Hel was a member of the royal family as well. Otherwise there would have been no other children to play with."

"D'Tierrza? You two are close?"

He nodded. "We always have been. A cousin makes a convenient best friend."

"It's good you two had each other."

He laughed. "I won't argue with that. Without my steadying influence, who knows where the woman would have ended up?"

Mina snorted. As Helene d'Tierrza had flouted every aristocratic convention and continued to cause controversy by holding her position in the Royal Guard, she had to wonder indeed.

The King smiled. "And, in answer to your earlier question, we take off when I get in there." He angled his head toward the cockpit.

She started. "You're flying us?"

The grin that flashed across his face at her astonishment was pure and light and worth every iota of uncertainty resting in her gut about putting her fate in the hands of a hobby pilot.

Anxiety stood no chance against the cocky ease in his expression. Its spark was like a snapshot to the past, undoubtedly more familiar to older versions of himself. Her heart thudded even as the right side of her brain demanded she collect more information.

"When did you learn how to fly?" she asked. Somehow it didn't seem politic for the nation's future King to have engaged in such a risky recreational activity.

His grin stretched wider, and she had the distinct impression that she was going to be even more shocked by his response.

"When I was fifteen."

"Fifteen?" Mina sputtered. "That can't be legal!"

He shrugged, obviously enjoying her shock, before asking insouciantly, "What's 'legal' to the King?"

"I should hope a lot. And you weren't the King then," she pointed out.

He shrugged. "What's legal to the Queen?"

"The Queen let you fly planes at fifteen?"

He laughed at the incredulity in her voice and nodded. "She did. Insisted, in fact."

"That doesn't seem very safe…"

Zayn tsked. "That's awfully judgmental of you, Dr. Aldaba."

She shook her head. "Reasonable. You were the only heir to the throne."

"As you are about to entrust your health and wellbeing to my flying, I'd have to beg to argue that it's incredibly safe. I never would have imagined that you, Dr. Amina Aldaba, youngest scholar ever nominated for the King's council and barrier-breaking pioneer, were so old-fashioned."

Instead of stinging, his words brought a smile to her face. He wasn't throwing her lost dreams in her face—he was teasing her. The idea filled her with an unfamiliar feeling of warmth.

"I am an excellent pilot, if you're worried," he added.

She looked up to meet his violet gaze, saying with complete honesty, "I have no doubt you are excellent at everything you do."

Her words hung in the suddenly charged air between them. She hadn't meant them as anything but a straightforward observation, but somehow, in the atmosphere of it being just she and the King together, the words throbbed with innuendo.

Clearing his throat, the King said, "Glad to know I have your confidence. Now, if we're ever going to arrive, I'd better get this bird in the air."

He left her in the cabin with a nod, heading into the cockpit and closing the door between them with a decisive click.

Mina took her seat and clicked the seat belt, though there was no light to indicate she needed to do so in the luxurious interior. Alone, without the presence of her husband to absorb her focus, she had more time to examine every element of takeoff.

Fortunately, their transition from thousands of pounds in weight of land-bound metal to weightless flying creature was buttery-smooth. Better, she had to acknowledge, than any commercial flight she'd ever been on.

The first twenty minutes of the flight were smooth and clear, with the island soon coming into sight. Sooner than she would have imagined. Given the height and angle of the plane to the island, and the lack of any visible infrastructure, she was surprised when they banked toward a gorgeous long stretch of sandy beach.

Her geometry was rusty, but a frown came to her brow as they began what felt like a descent right on to the beach. There was no runway in sight.

She entered the cockpit to find the King ramrod-straight in the pilot's seat, gripping the wheel with what was surely an unnecessary amount of muscle. His neck was tense and his entire being was focused on guiding the plane toward the beach ahead of them.

She looked once more from the King to the beach, and then back to the King again.

"We're having to make an emergency landing on that beach, aren't we?" she asked as if she had been asking about the weather. Her nerves felt strangely numb as she took in the situation, while her mind, well-muscled and rigorously disciplined, processed the data.

"We are."

He didn't look at her. He shouldn't and she didn't really want him to. She wanted him to land the plane. With all her heart, as it turned out. It took only one stark moment for her to realize that she wanted her life—even if it consisted of tattered dreams and ill-suited roles.

"I was afraid of that." She was far too calm for the situation going on around them. She recognized that, and knew that it suggested she was in shock. In a mild haze, she asked, "What can I do?"

He shook his head. "Nothing. It appears our engine has stalled, so unless by chance you have some knowledge of aerospace engineering, I suggest you sit tight." He spoke sarcastically, though his forearms flexed against the plane's yoke.

Mina nodded. She did not, so she sat calmly in the co-pilot's seat, closed and adjusted her seatbelt, and was still. Searching for something to hold on to, her hand found the King's thigh, and she squeezed as she watched the rapid approach of the long beach of rich chocolate-brown sand.

At what felt like the last possible moment, he straightened the plane, lifting its nose just enough to bring the wheels into jarring contact with sand, rather than the front end of the plane. They skidded to a halt, the plane's front end digging huge tracks into the beach but miraculously holding its shape and integrity.

"Are you all right?" the King asked, once the noise and dust had settled around them.

After her breath returned, Mina nodded.

"Thank God." The words came out on an exhale, along with the unspoken message that he'd been far more uncertain about landing than he'd projected.

Taking a deep breath, Mina said, "I'm glad you know how to fly planes."

The King let out a shaky laugh. "Me too." But he was back to business quickly. "Now, I hope you're ready to walk. It's about a half-day's trek through the woodlands to get to the cabin, and then another couple of hours of pretty steep hiking from there to get to the summer palace, as the crow flies."

Mina nodded. After surviving an emergency plane landing, she could handle a half-day hike through gentle woodlands.

"Leave your luggage here for now—just worry about water. The cabin is stocked, as is the summer palace. The clean-up team will collect what's here."

"Won't they be looking for us at the plane?"

"I sent them a message in my SOS. They know we're heading to the cabin rather than waiting. This beach is inaccessible via land vehicle, and we do not have any ship large enough nearby to handle carrying the plane, so it will take hours for the crew to get organized."

He was up and moving, grabbing items from the cabin as he spoke, and soon Mina had no choice but to follow the King across the beach and into the woods.

CHAPTER SIX

"TAKE OFF THE sweater," Zayn said through clenched teeth, waiting for an obviously overheated Mina to catch up once again.

While the wild woods of Cantorini were renowned in the region for their density, they remained Mediterranean woodlands, comprised of a mixture of oaks and mixed sclerophylls. It was an infinitely traversable landscape, even if the rocky terrain was brutal on the ankles. But not if one was wearing a wool sweater more appropriate for a winter evening by the sea than a warm summer walk through the woods.

"Excuse me, I will not," she insisted.

It was the same thing she'd said each time he'd made the demand, but this time he was going to make her do it. He was the King, after all. It was his prerogative to order people to do things.

Her cheeks had a rosy flush to them that had nothing to do with her reaction to him, and her skin glistened with perspiration. He wasn't having it. She had only a few more miles in her before heatstroke set in, and they had more miles than that before they'd reach the cabin.

Rather than repeat the order, he simply began to unbutton his own shirt.

Mina's green gaze widened. "What are you doing?"

"Giving you my shirt."

"What?"

"You're going to wear my shirt."

"I couldn't," she said, shaking her head.

"I insist," he ground out, his irritation at being resisted growing with every button he freed.

"Absolutely not."

"If it requires my tearing that atrocious sweater off your body with my bare hands, I absolutely insist."

"You wouldn't dare," she challenged.

"As that eyesore has been burning itself into my mind's eye since the early hours of this morning, I can assure you I would. Quite happily."

He said the last with a growl in his voice and Mina took a step back.

Fighting the urge to roll his eyes, he said, "I'm the King, Mina. Not a murderer. You're going to get heatstroke if you don't take off the damn sweater."

She stared at him mutinously and he prepared for another refusal, inwardly curious at the idea of making good on his word. The image of relieving her of her clothing, albeit with more finesse than she was likely expecting, lent itself to all kinds of intriguing conclusions.

But it wasn't to be.

"Turn around," she said.

He raised an eyebrow. "Really, Mina? We've just survived an emergency plane landing, we're alone in the woods, and we're married."

She set her jaw and nodded.

"You're a child," he said, turning.

Behind him, she muttered under her breath, "Just because I'm not an exhibitionist like everyone else around here…"

He found himself smiling. And that in itself was unexpected. After starting his day with the punch to the solar plexus that had been Mina fresh in the morning, and closing it out by crash landing his favorite plane on a heretofore pristine beach, he wouldn't have thought he could muster the mood for a smile.

Stealing a quick glance over his shoulder, though, he caught a flash of Mina's golden-brown skin before it disappeared beneath the black of his shirt and realized he could do more than smile. The glimpse was over before he'd barely had time to register it, and banally chaste at that, yet his mouth watered. The heat that raced through him was the same heat that had overtaken him when she had been in his arms the night before.

Had it only been the night before when he'd kissed her for the first time? He'd have to add bending time to her list of uncanny abilities, this stranger who was his wife. In the short time he'd known her she had been transformed, and yet he realized now that the packaging was entirely superficial when it came to this woman. The core essence of her remained, no matter what she wore, and at her core she was the same woman he'd encountered in the chapel at their first meeting.

The thought had him stealing another glance at her.

She walked deliberately, her eyes continuously scanning the scenery. His shirt was large on her, though her breasts appeared to be doing their best to fill it out, and it occurred to him that it wasn't fair to other women to have such a brilliant mind wrapped up in all that delicious packaging.

They fell into sync, making their way through the woodlands, walking side by side, with Mina occasionally stopping to examine a particular plant or sign of wildlife, and Zayn tolerating the delays long enough for her to make a quick note in her pocket memo pad before he drove them onward.

On one particularly exuberant occasion she stopped, gasping and pointing a waggling finger over his shoulder as a series of strange squeals escaped her throat.

Zayn whipped around to catch a rustle in the underbrush and the sound of something scurrying away. Turning back to Mina, he waited for her to catch her breath.

"It was a brown-beaked warbler!"

He smiled. The brown-beaked warbler was one of the endemic species on the island. He'd seen them before, having taken countless trips to the island over the course of his life, but her excitement was catching nonetheless—like watching a child at Christmas.

"To just happen upon one!" she gushed. "What are the chances?"

Her color was up, and so bright that not even the black of his shirt could diminish her glow, and he realized that, despite the circumstances, he was enjoying this time with her. In a way he couldn't remember enjoying anything since becoming King.

It was hard to truly enjoy things after losing your father, learning that your uncle had been behind the plot that killed him, saying goodbye to your mother, because her home had become a house of mirrors filled with the ghost of her husband, hiding it all, and then assuming the throne—all within a year and a half. And yet here he was, enjoying himself nonetheless.

As they continued their hike Mina grew bolder, pointing out more and more flora and fauna as if she were leading a tour group. None of the information was new to him, the island having been in his family for the last hundred years or so, but her enthusiasm charmed him. With every step, the combination of her earnest exuberance and being back on the island seemed to shake off some of the weight of the past two years.

And she had no idea.

"What exactly is your field of study?" he asked, suddenly feeling the gulf of his lack of knowledge about her.

She frowned, eyeing him suspiciously. "I'm a biological systems scientist. Or rather, I was…" This last she'd added with a frown and a note of confusion.

The uncertainty in her voice roused in him an urge to conquer and destroy, but her identity crisis wasn't an enemy he could fight. She could thank their fathers for that.

"You are still," he said, trying anyway. "Becoming Queen does not negate your years of study."

She sent him a nod, accompanied by a vague smile, and he had the unusual experience of realizing she was humoring him.

"It doesn't," he insisted, more determined in the face of her brush-off.

"Of course not. I know that."

She put more effort into her smile, and it occurred to him that the expression would likely have fooled anyone who wasn't looking closely.

He *was* looking closely. "But...?" he asked.

She sighed. "But what does a queen need a PhD in biological systems for?"

He was still searching for an answer when she distracted him once again.

"Look! Another warbler. A female, I think."

He obediently turned in the direction she pointed and smiled when he caught sight of the small, unassuming brown head.

"Females are even more difficult to spot than males," she squealed. "We're lucky we're here at the beginning of the mating season."

"You know quite a lot about our little warblers."

She shook her head. "Not the warbler, actually. Just this particular bio-system. I was the only scholar at the university in over a decade to focus on Cyranese ecosystems. It was never as sexy as studying the famous ones, like the Great Barrier Reef or the Amazon, but my father always encouraged me to value my home and work for 'the good of Cyrano...'"

Her voice trailed off as they both followed the thought to its conclusion.

Her father's meaning and motivation were clear

now, and they both knew that he had gone far beyond simply being an encouraging parent, but for the first time Zayn didn't resent the man.

"It certainly doesn't hurt for a monarch to have a deep understanding of the nation in their charge."

She cringed, saying, "You don't have to pretend when it's just the two of us. We both know I'm no monarch."

Zayn raised a brow. "I believe there's a small island nation which would disagree."

Instead of rising to his bait, she doubled down. "But we both know I'm a fraud."

"How do you come to say that?" he asked.

"I'm a scholar. Not a queen."

"As far as I understand, being a queen entails inheriting or marrying into a throne—the second of which you have done."

"I'm an imposter."

He didn't reply, scanning the scrub and the grasses that covered the ground around them, and smiling when he saw a cluster of the plants he was looking for. Four small stalks stuck out of the ground, each bearing leaves of shiny dark green, growing in sets of three. Crouching down, he reached toward the plants on the left.

Mina opened her mouth to protest and he stopped, his finger just inches from the leaves.

"The wax leaf sand thistle. Now, here is an

imposter," he said. "As I'm sure you know, Dr. Aldaba, this plant nefariously mimics its companion here, the wax leaf sugar sap, growing in the same conditions and showcasing almost identical foliage. But, whereas the wax leaf sugar sap is both a delectable treat for the spotted fallow deer that live on the island, and an important nitrogen fixer for the soil, the wax leaf sand thistle is bitter to the deer and known for stripping the earth. It mimics the sugar sap for its own benefit—using the deer to spread its seeds, while offering them nothing but a stinging mouth in return." He rocked back on his heels before adding, "We don't know each other well, Mina, but I don't get the impression that you are a person out to take without giving back."

Leaning back further, to take her in, he noted the cracks in her inscrutable expression, her desire to believe him warring with her natural skepticism.

When her eyes widened and rounded, he thought desire had won out—until she shouted, "Watch out!" just before he felt a sharp stinging pain in the fleshy side of his palm as his hand brushed too close to the thistle.

The burn of it was immediate—another feature of the sand thistle was its shockingly powerful prick, often likened to that of a bee sting.

Mina acted instantly, dropping her pack to

crouch down and begin searching the under-growth. Zayn distracted himself from the swelling throb in his hand by watching her move. It didn't matter that he had no idea what she was doing, or that she wore baggy jeans and his shirt, there was something erotic about her in that position.

She found whatever she was looking for with an, "Aha!" and was at his side an instant later. "Give me your hand."

Her command was absolute. She had no thought that she might be disobeyed, and he found a silly half-grin lifting the corner of his mouth at her authority, even through the discomfort of obliging her.

She shoved the bunch of leaves he now saw she had collected into her mouth and chewed, before slapping the gooey mess on the place where his hand had made contact with the thistle.

Instantly the pain subsided. A small sound of pleasure escaped him, and he didn't know if the expressive slip-up had more to do with the sudden absence of discomfort, the fact that being on the island was like going back in time to an era when he hadn't had to manage his every move, or the fact that Mina had just made him feel good.

Her answering smile glowed with relief. "Systems science. Antidotes to the toxins that have evolved in a given environment can almost always be found nearby."

If she'd still been wearing her glasses, he imagined this would have been the moment she pushed them up the bridge of her nose, but there was no derision in the thought. Her earnestness wasn't the cluelessness of a sheltered academic. She was just genuine.

He came to his feet to hide just how that revelation hit him, and composed himself before offering her a hand. "And you said a queen had no use for a PhD in biological systems…"

After a slight hesitation, and looking at his offered hand for a beat too long, she accepted it, letting him carry some of her weight as she came upright.

"Thanks," she said, when they both stood again.

Her green-hazel eyes mirrored the color of the forest around them as she stared at him, revealing herself in the process, as natural and forthright as the woods.

She stole his breath, but she didn't seem to care that that gave her power—maybe she didn't even know it.

Heat was coming to her cheeks at their continued eye contact, and she cleared her throat. "Well, should we keep going?"

Watching her trying to hide her reaction to him

filled him with an unfamiliar urge to beat his chest and let out a wild howl. And even though the movement wouldn't have been like any version of himself—not the island-exploring boy, not the passionate student, not the charming heir, and certainly not the King—he realized it came from the same place that made a man hunt and kill and die for his woman. It didn't matter what version he was of himself. This part was his real essence.

It wasn't a comfortable realization.

He wasn't, however, about to wallow in his mind's damning over-simplifications. The real world offered intrigue enough.

Unlike his present company.

The more time he spent with her, the more he realized she couldn't offer intrigue if her life depended on it. However her father had managed to secure a royal betrothal so long ago, his daughter didn't appear to have a machinating bone in her body.

"Tell me about your mother?" he asked, curious to know if her earnestness stemmed from another source.

"Do you know you're quite bossy?" she retorted, rather than answering his question.

He raised an eyebrow. "I ask about your mother and you resort to name-calling?"

She snorted with a little laugh, watching the ground as she walked, at complete ease, and he realized he couldn't remember the last time some-one had snorted around him.

He tried again. "Will you tell me about your mother?"

She laughed out loud this time. "Even when you use the right words you can't really ask for anything, can you?"

She sparkled, and he marveled at her while she teased him as if he wasn't the King.

Glancing at him out the side of her eye, she asked slyly, "Don't you have some sort of dossier on me?"

Taking on the challenge in her question, he shrugged. "Of course. Your mother was born in Germany and came to Cyrano on a student visa. She dropped out of school and illegally outstayed her visa, during which time she met your father. They married, and through your father—who was a natural-born citizen and had been a military officer—earned her citizenship."

Her eyes had widened into small green gold orbs in her face and he laughed.

"But what is that? Facts? I want to know what my mother-in-law is like."

He really was curious about the mother-in-law he had yet to meet, but he couldn't remember the last time he had been able to laugh at his plans going awry. Mina, however, was unaware of that—completely oblivious to the fact that she and the island were drawing out parts of himself he'd thought long dead—and she laughed, the sound of it as bright as the sun overhead.

"When you put it that way…"

Her voice carried her smile with it, right into his chest, where it blossomed like a hothouse flower.

"She is a devoted mother, and so strong—she had to be after we lost my father—"

The ghost of pain in her voice was a quiet echo of the raw-edged thing that lived inside him, usually clawing its way up to the surface from the deep place where he had buried it the moment he let himself slow down, and in a strange way it was both comforting and hopeful.

"I could have easily fallen into a depression after that, but she wouldn't let me. She said that he was alive as long as I kept his dreams alive in my heart, and she encouraged me to keep getting up every day, to keep studying and trying, and not to just lie down and give up forever."

"Somehow, I don't picture that ever happening," he said, an image of her squaring her shoulders in the chapel coming to his mind. "You would have gotten back up eventually—though perhaps she was right to push you. Watching someone you love collapse in grief is…hard."

She searched his face before asking, "Your mother?"

Irritated by the pinch her soft question set off in his chest, he answered with a short nod. "For a time it looked like I might lose her as well as my father. Ultimately she had to leave, so it didn't matter that she'd got back up. I lost her anyway."

A thousand questions flashed across her eyes, but she only asked one. "What do you mean, she had to leave?"

Like a terrier, she had grabbed hold of the one thing he'd said with the greatest implication for matters of state. Matters that had not been made public and that he had no intention of ever making so.

And he'd thought her mind was only suited to science. She just might learn to be Queen after all. And, though he'd been enjoying the unfamiliar lightness of their conversation, he didn't resent this, her inevitable intrusion into his personal life, as it was an opportunity to test her as Queen.

Carefully, he said with casualness, "She was the true target of the assassination."

Mina stopped in her tracks, completely guileless in her shock. "What? Why does no one know this?"

"Many details around the assassination are classified."

"Did she leave because she was afraid?"

He laughed, "My mother? That woman has never been afraid a day in her life." He shook his head. "No. She left because ours is a small island. My father's memory was everywhere for her, and guilt and grief were killing her."

"I can understand… But this way it's like you've lost two parents at once."

Her eyes oozed pain for him and he frowned, not liking the way her empathy felt like a balm. "Now, Mina. Don't be maudlin. You know there is nothing like losing a parent but losing a parent."

The bite in his retort had exactly the effect he had been going for. The sympathetic light in her eye dimmed, replaced with a hint of fire.

He continued, "But, as you now know the full story, you must indulge my desire to learn more about the new mother figure in *my* life."

Mina rolled her eyes, but it was a sham to cover up the heart pouring out of them. "I don't know how I would have made it through without my mother. We adore each other. I have dinner with her two nights a week, usually, and typically stay over on those nights."

"Interesting…" Zayn noted. "I hadn't observed that."

Mina laughed, once again righting the world with the sound of joy.

"Well, not lately. She's been wanting to take an extended holiday back home in Germany—my grandparents are getting older, you know—and when I learned of my parliamentary interview we both knew I'd be focused on preparing, so she decided to take her trip now. She's due back midsummer. We'd planned to take a spa weekend together, either to celebrate or soothe, depending on the outcome…"

Her voice trailed off and they both thought of what the outcome had been—something far different from what Mina and her mother had imagined.

Zayn vowed in that moment to make sure Mina's time at the summer palace made up for the spa weekend she'd missed. He couldn't reinstate her position on the council—a queen could not sit on the council—and he couldn't give her back her life as a professor and researcher, but he could at least give her back one of the plans her marriage to him had taken from her.

Her pampering would begin the moment they arrived at the summer palace. But they had to get there first.

"We're about thirty minutes from the cabin," he said. "We can make it there before we lose the light. From there it's less than two hours' walk to the summer palace, but for that we can wait for daylight."

Mina nodded. "I'm ready if you are."

Once again he set the pace, and Mina kept up, this time forgoing any observation notes, and as the last creeping tendrils of light faded on the horizon they stepped suddenly out of the woods into the clearing that housed the palatial log cabin.

Constructed of thick old logs, and large polished stones, the building was designed in a traditional lodge style, with large, scenic picture windows in the center of two outstretched, smooth-timbered wings. Two-storied, it was a commanding structure, made all the more so by the fact that it was the first evidence of mankind they had encountered in miles.

"The cabin is kept stocked with supplies at all times. But unfortunately, it has yet to be retrofitted with satellite services, so we won't be able to call from it. It should meet our needs for the night, though."

Mina merely nodded as he opened the door, gasping when she stepped inside.

Smiling at her wonder, Zayn took in the large exposed beams of the ceiling, the plushly accented open spaces and the enormous central fireplace with nonchalance. "I always thought it was rather rustic and a bit too cozy myself..."

Mina laughed. "I'm sure. After all, no satellite services..."

She wandered round the expansive living area first and then the large kitchen, noting the locations of necessary items as she opened cabinets and drawers.

"Oh, and here's a can opener! Perfect!"

"A can opener?" He raised an eyebrow.

Mina's owlish look alone would have been comical, but when it was coupled with her next words he had trouble keeping a straight face.

"You *do* know that people eat food out of cans, right?" she asked delicately, and her attempt to disguise exactly what she would think about him if he answered no was almost painful.

Holding back, he nodded seriously. "I am aware."

Her sigh of relief was too much, though, and it broke the dam on his laughter.

When he could breathe again, he wiped the tears from the corners of his eyes and offered, "I may be King, but I still had my uni days."

She rolled her eyes at that. "I'm sure…"

"What's that supposed to mean?"

Grinning, she shrugged. "Somehow I imagine your late-night takeout and pajama days were a bit higher-class than mine."

It was his turn to shrug, his smile easy. "Probably. But caviar still comes out of a can."

This time it was she who couldn't hold back, and the laughter rolled out of her with a faint edge of hysteria to it—the only hint at the unusual day she'd had. He was impressed.

"Whether it's out of a can, or anything else, we should eat and then rest up," he said. "We can shower and change and set out early tomorrow. If we're lucky, we'll be at the summer palace before lunch."

Sobering, she nodded. "I don't have a change of clothes, but a shower sounds divine. Or, even better yet, a long soak…"

She virtually purred at the idea, her voice going husky and smooth, and despite crash landing his plane and an unplanned half-day hike, he felt his pants tighten in response.

"Ask and you shall receive," he said. "The summer palace is always stocked with spare clothing and the master bath is equipped with a state-of-the-art hot tub and, I believe, every kind of bath salt and soaking serum anyone could want."

Closing her eyes, she let out a long, contented sigh, before her eyes shot open again. "Do you know how to cook?"

He almost answered honestly—the question as ridiculous as her concern about canned food—but held back at the last second, curious to see how she would respond.

Keeping his face carefully blank, he said, "I know how a can opener works."

Frowning, she said, "That's not very self-sufficient—but unsurprising. When would you have had to cook? It's fine, though. I can put something together for us. It won't be what you're used to—I'm no chef—but we won't starve." She eyed him through the corner of her eye, apparently content with her own answers to her questions. "And it will be more than a heated up can of green beans…"

Not bothering to correct her impression, he smiled openly. "Wonderful. I can't say I was looking forward to green beans…"

He did, however, find he was looking forward to having her cook for him. He might be used to top-rated chefs, but something about the idea set off something hot and primal inside him.

"After dinner, though, that bath has my name all over it."

Her grin could only be described as wolfish, but he found himself attracted to its wild greed, wanting to see the same glint reflected in her eyes when she took him in. Preferably in the bath, her body naked and slick…

His body stirred again, and, with the direction his thoughts were taking, he decided it was time for a shower himself. An ice-cold one.

Entering the brightly lit and expansively marbled bathroom, he reflected on the fact that his concept of "cozy" was relative. At ten thousand square feet, the cabin certainly wasn't small, and it boasted every modern comfort. But, most importantly, it was private.

The time he'd spent here with his parents was the only time he could remember in all his life when they'd had no servants or staff dancing attendance. His father had insisted on it after the renovation. His son might have been a prince, but he was going to experience life without being waited on hand and foot.

Removing his pants and putting them in the hidden hamper, Zayn then turned the shower on. Steaming jets burst forth from the wall and the waterfall showerhead, stinging his skin as the water encountered the small cuts and abrasions he'd picked up from trekking shirtless through the woods. He hadn't noticed amassing them on the way. He had been too engrossed in Mina.

Electricity lit his veins at the thought of her. The two of them were absolutely alone, with no staff present to witness any lapses in decorum. Any uncontrolled response would be private...a secret shared between him and his wife.

With her downstairs, preparing dinner for the two of them while he showered, he could almost pretend they were ordinary people—a regular man and woman settling down for the evening, rather than a king and a queen with responsibilities to put their nation before their own happiness. He could almost imagine that they were united by common ground and shared desire, rather than by merely being the casualties of an antiquated contractual agreement.

He turned off the shower and pulled a plush towel from the tidily stacked pile to wrap around his waist. Exiting the bathroom, he was greeted by the scent of North African spices, drawing his attention to his gnawing hunger. Whether he was starving for sustenance or the woman behind the delectable combination of aromas, however, he wasn't sure.

He followed the scent downstairs and into the kitchen, to find Mina standing in front of the stove with her back to him.

She still wore her jeans and his shirt, the hem of which hit her mid-thigh and hung loosely. The jeans beneath it certainly weren't cut to showcase the female form, yet the image of what lay beneath was so clear in his mind it was as if he could see through every layer of clothing.

More curls had escaped the loose bun she'd started the day with, but the effect sat well with her masculine attire, hinting at the vibrant femininity that lay beneath. And below that her dizzying intellect. What lay below that he could only guess at, though each layer he discovered seemed more powerful and awe-inspiring than the last.

He could spend a lifetime delving into her depths and never run out of new facets to explore... The idea brought unfamiliar warmth to his chest.

He knew the moment she became aware of his presence, though she didn't turn around. It was as if a pulse of electricity travelled through her body, until she thrummed with a kind of tension that invited him closer.

"The kitchen is really well stocked," she said. "We had everything I needed for my grandma's chicken tagine."

She kept her voice over-bright, and he knew she was trying to settle her response to him. Not wanting that, he stepped further into the kitchen, standing only a few feet away now as she continued to cook.

When he spoke, he let his smile spill into the words. "Definitely better than a heated can of green beans. Smells delicious."

And even though she kept her back to him he could sense the blush of pleasure that heated her skin. Could hear it in the catch of her breath.

"Thank you. You're lucky. It's about one of ten dishes I know how to make, and it is by far the best."

Warm laughter rumbled in his chest, rising up out of him from a place far different from the presentational mirth he normally put on. Unbidden, an image of his father rose in his mind. Of the three of them, in fact—his father, mother, and himself—together in this very kitchen, his father at the stove, joking, he and his mother sitting at the counter, his rapt audience.

He was sure he hadn't recalled that evening since it had happened, which had to be at least fifteen years before, because there was nothing remarkable about it. And yet there the memory was, crystal-clear after all these years.

"Almost done here." Mina's voice shone through the bittersweet thoughts, and she said over her shoulder, "Do you mind setting the table?"

He almost laughed.

The question had been so natural and innocuous, delivered off-hand from one person to another. For a brief moment, at least, she'd forgotten that he was the King. It was a novel experience—one he rather liked.

She turned off the stove and finally turned around, opening her mouth to speak as she moved.

But whatever she had been about to say was lost when she abruptly snapped her mouth shut, eyes going wide. "I'm sorry. I didn't realize you weren't dressed. I'll set the table."

He did laugh this time, the sound low and heated. Still smiling, he said, "I'll get dressed after dinner. I'd be happy to set the table."

She licked her lips, and although his groin tightened in response, threatening the stability of the towel, he was certain she was unaware of the action.

Her cheeks had a rosy sheen to them, and there was a light in her eyes that hadn't been there

moments before, but rather than take any steps
down the path of seduction, she clapped her hands
together and said in an overloud voice, "Great.
Thanks." Before reaching for, and knocking over,
the container of wooden serving spoons that sat
on the counter.

Sure that his laughter would not be abating any
time soon, Zayn decided to give her a break, gathering the silverware to set the table as his lady
had requested.

CHAPTER SEVEN

IT HAD TO be shock. Shock that was setting in after a day that had begun with her first hangover, included a plane crash, and was now coming to a close with a disorienting coziness that felt almost normal—albeit on a rather larger scale than most people could afford.

Considering the last few weeks of her life, any hint of normalcy would be reason enough for her to go into shock. So that was what was happening. That was why her temperature had spiked when she'd turned to see Zayn's broad chest, clean and gleaming, a plush low-slung towel wrapped around his waist the only barrier between her eyes and his full naked glory.

Shock was why her breasts had gone heavy and tender when he'd stepped closer to her in the kitchen, and her imagination had supplied her with the sensation of his breath against the back of her neck, his body heat radiating outward to envelop her.

Shock was behind the growing heat at her core—not the King.

Her body was short-circuiting from a system overload, rather than due to the arousal the biologist in her demanded that she acknowledge. She was a mammal, after all. She couldn't help her body's natural response to being confronted with the perfection that was her King.

Golden and muscled, his chest was sprinkled with light hair that disappeared around his gorgeous pectorals and didn't reappear again until it formed the line that began below his navel and disappeared beneath the towel.

Mina swallowed.

She had seen the naked human form before, but never like this. Never so visceral and hot and alive. Never so commanding. Never so cut.

It had been hard enough to focus during their hours of hiking, when only his chest had been exposed. There was no way she would make it through dinner knowing he had nothing on under the towel.

What would her grandmother think of her wild thoughts? How could she sit at a table and eat her grandmother's recipe while her mind took off on a carnal tear, presenting her with crisp images of kissing a trail from his jaw all the way down his chest and along that oh-so-kindly marked path she'd observed.

She was going to combust while he laid out utensils on the table.

Human immolation was rare, but scientifically possible, given the right conditions. And the growing internal inferno that threatened to engulf her entire body seemed like the right conditions.

Shoving her hands into oven mitts, at this point more to protect the pan from her heat than the other way round, she carried the dish to the trivet Zayn had laid on the table.

"Mina…" His voice was a seductive caress. "That looks delicious."

Since it wasn't possible to blush any more than she already was, Mina tried playing it cool as she joined him at the table. "Thank you. It helps to have such high-quality ingredients."

Zayn smiled and her toes curled in her socks.

"My dad used to say the same thing," he said.

His dad. King Alden. She wondered if she would ever get used to such casual references to royalty. But to Zayn, the royal family wasn't the pinnacle of the aristocracy. It was just family.

"Your father cooked?" she asked, placing the serving spoon and turning to collect the rice and the teff. Zayn had chosen the small dining nook for their dinner, and Mina was grateful. The large table she'd seen in the dining room reminded her too much of breakfast.

"He did," he said. And after a beat, he added, "He insisted I learn as well."

Mina snorted. "You call heating up a can of vegetables cooking?"

He shrugged. "Your words, not mine."

She raised an eyebrow at him. "You're telling me you know how to cook?"

"Don't sound so surprised."

"What can you make?"

She couldn't picture Zayn in a kitchen outside of the image he presented now, sitting at the table, shirtless.

"Simple things. *Pesce al grappa, polle al grappa, paella, polle dominga, jamon e quez...*"

Mina was impressed with the list. It was classic Cyranese cooking, much of it considered common food, but all the more delicious for it.

But rather than tell him that she said, "Well, next time you're cooking, then."

He smiled, and in the intimate lighting of the nook it lit his face with ease. "Gladly. I would love to feed you."

His words carried promises far beyond those of a shared meal and Mina shivered.

"Did your mother cook?" she asked.

Zayn chuckled, shaking his head slightly. "No. The noble Singuenza daughters were not allowed anywhere near the kitchens during their formative years and later it was always beyond my mother. I imagine it's the same for Aunt Seraphina. She was never the rebel."

"I hear the sound of family stories there." Mina leaned in, observing her own ease for the first time she could remember in months—certainly since long before she'd learned of her parliamentary interview.

He lifted his hands, palms up to her. "You'll have to ask my mother yourself. Everything I know I learned secondhand from my cousin Helene, who learned it piecemeal from her mother. There are rumors that my mother was quite the wild child in her youth, though."

"Queen Barbara? Absolutely not. She is dignity personified."

Zayn lifted an eyebrow. "You buy the image? For shame, Mina."

She laughed. "Well, I'll just have to ask the source."

"What about you? Do you have any wild stories from your youth?"

She knew a frown flashed across her face at his words, but it was gone as soon as it appeared.

"Not me," she said, with a self-deprecating smile. "I really just studied. Nothing exciting about my past—I'm just your average citizen."

Zayn snorted. "I find that hard to believe. You were about to be appointed to the King's council, you speak multiple languages, you've been to Ecuador on a research expedition. That's a lot more than the average citizen."

Mina smiled. "When you put it like that…"

He laughed, and she wondered if he knew that the low rumble of that sound was the key to the lock that kept the heat of her core at bay.

"I do," he insisted.

He was iron and charm, threaded together through both King and man, and the combination created a powerful magnetism.

Heat bloomed in her cheeks, her breath catching a bit as she said, "Well, it takes a lot of study to do those things, which doesn't leave much time for wild stories."

He raised an eyebrow. "In my experience, wild stories make time for themselves."

The heat in Mina's cheeks took on a different nature at his words. Wild stories, it would seem, had just purposely avoided her then—because she had none. She had stories of falling asleep with her nose in a book, and spending her rare free nights tucked away in her mother's living room. All to keep alive the memory of a man she apparently hadn't ever really known.

"Not even a love affair to distract from your focus?" he asked.

She shook her head in response. "Not even a love affair, I'm afraid. Just boring study, night after night." She blushed again. She hadn't meant to say that, emphasizing that her nights all the rest of the life she had spent alone. She took a sip of her water to wash down the knot of embarrassment lodged in her throat.

"It sounds like you're ripe for something wild, then."

His tone implied that he was open to being the one to introduce wild into her life, and she choked on her water before trying to brush it off as a chuckle.

"Ha-ha." She enunciated the sound as if she was new to the process of laughter, before adding, "The only thing I'm ripe for is a bath."

He shook his head, amusement alive in his eyes, but simply said, "I can handle the dishes, Mina. Go upstairs and take your bath."

She didn't wait for him to say it twice. Making her way into the living room, it was impossible for her to miss the gorgeous wide staircase that led to the second floor. Taking it, she wandered the hallways, every now and then stealing a glance down through the open-plan living room into the kitchen to see Zayn in his towel.

It occurred to her that the towel was the first thing she'd seen him wear that wasn't black. A bubble of laughter escaped at the thought, and the edge to its sound reminded her that, regardless of how relaxed things were now, she'd pushed her body past its limits over the course of the day.

Away from Zayn's temperature-raising presence, the aches and pains of the day made themselves felt. And why shouldn't they? She had drunk and danced late into the night the night before, been woken up too early, with a hangover, survived an emergency plane landing, and gone on a four-hour hike within the last twenty-four hours. It was a wonder she was even upright at this point. A hot bath and a date with a pillow were exactly what the doctor ordered.

Offset from the other doors, at the far end of the long upper hallway, was a pair of large French doors. The master suite, if she had to guess and, she suspected, the location of the hot tub.

Inside, the bedroom was bright, plush, and clean. A massive bed covered with a well-stuffed white duvet demanded attention, but it didn't begin to dominate the enormous room. Much like the Queen's Suite at the palace, small archways led form it to what she assumed were closets and additional rooms.

Moments later, she squealed with delight to find the bathroom.

She searched the cabinets, gleeful when she discovered a gratuitous selection of luxury bath salts and balms. She turned the water on in the tub while reading the package labels. Settling on a combination of relaxation and muscle-soothing, she added the salts and quickly peeled off her clothes, before stepping over the high edge of tub and into heaven on earth.

A moan slipped free from her lips as she sank in, feeling hot jets of water working her tender muscles the whole time.

The tub was everything Zayn had promised and more—deep, powerful, big enough to drown in—and she couldn't have designed it better in her imagination.

"Mmm…" Her hum of pleasure was unstoppable.

For the first time since she'd left her apartment for her interview, weeks ago, she was completely alone. The relief that came with that was more profound than she would have believed possible before meeting the King.

She closed her eyes and leaned back, thinking there was a real chance she might fall asleep in the tub. Slowly inhaling the lavender and eucalyptus combination of the bath salts, she bent her mind to the task of relaxing, beginning at the crown of her head and working her way down, part by part. By the time she reached her toes her mind floated in a Zen haze, lulled into stillness by aromatherapy and hot water.

In that state, Zayn's image formed in her mind.

A smile curved her lips.

In her imagination he rose from a steaming spring, the same broad chest she'd barely been able to tear her eyes from all day glistening with beads of heated water that begged to be traced with her tongue. As usual, his violet gaze burned, but this time the fire was fueled by desire—and all of it for her.

She shivered in the tub, despite the heat of the water. There was an undeniable thrill that came with the image. To have the King burn for her...

The bathroom door hinges creaked and Mina shot up, her eyes popping open, arms crossing in front of her breasts.

Zayn stood in the doorway, his movement halted mid-entry.

Their eyes met—hers wide and bright, and her cheeks flushed from more than the heat of the water, his piercing and focused, entirely zeroed in on her.

He cleared his throat. "I apologize. I was looking for my clothes. They are not in my old room."

Swallowing, Mina nodded, not trusting her ability to find words.

Entering the bathroom, he made his way toward the closet in the corner with gentlemanly decorum, not glancing toward the tub as he passed, and though she didn't know what else she could have wanted, Mina was disappointed.

He turned to leave with equal restraint, a folded black T-shirt and black cotton pants in his hands.

Mina watched his back as he walked toward

the door, a heavy sense of urgency growing in her chest. His hand was on the door handle when she called his name.

"Zayn."

He turned, meeting her eyes without a word.

Mina lowered her arms and the air left the room.

Time was transformed, racing as Zayn's eyes locked with hers to rip an irrefutable confirmation of her invitation from her at light-speed even while it slowed, going still as they sensed the invisible precipice they stood on.

And then he was moving toward her, a predator gone beyond stalking his prey, ready to pounce.

Her throat caught. She was suddenly nervous, but not enough. Not nearly enough. Not when they were alone in the cabin. Not when they were man and wife, their union not just sanctioned but sanctified. Certainly not when his eyes burned with an intensity that put her imagination to shame.

Her life's dream had been revealed to be a sham. Her academic reputation was in tatters. There was no more research to complete, no more grants to apply for. No more benchmarks to reach. She could make up no more excuses or distractions from taking a chance on real life—not when her husband was looking at her like that.

She stood, wearing only the water that ran down her skin.

The King stilled, not frozen but hyper-aware, his attention locked.

And then he was on her, closing the distance between them and cupping the back of her skull in his hands as he lifted her face towards his to take her mouth.

Her breasts pressed against the bare skin of his chest, her pebbled nipples exploding into sensation on contact. He snaked his arm around her waist, bracing her as he pulled her closer, pressing the hard length of his body against hers.

Held fast in his arms, she gave herself fully into the kiss, her senses wide open, etching each feeling into her memory. A hungry, desperate voice in the back of her mind was urging her on, warning her that this might be her only opportunity to feel this way.

Blood rushed through her, each vessel a river of heat coalescing at her core.

His hand found her breast, and the faintly roughened skin of his fingertips and palms against her skin was the most sensuous contrast she'd ever experienced. She arched into his grip, her breath catching in her throat.

The movement elicited a painful groan from him before he took her nipple between his thumb and forefinger. Rolling it gently, he experimented with pressure, watching her face intently as he set off mini waves of electric pleasure through her system.

She gasped when he replaced his fingers with his mouth, swirling his tongue around the sensitive hard bud. A moan of protest escaped her as he transitioned to the other breast, and she was bereft until he once again took her in his mouth.

Her fingers raked through his hair, thrilling in the silky texture she'd wanted to touch since seeing its midnight sheen up close in the chapel, and she had the strong urge to lift her legs and wrap them around his waist, press the burning heat at the juncture of her thighs closer to him.

Reading her mind, he scraped a palm down her back, over the curve of her behind, then down along the outer edge of her thigh to cup the back of her knee, drawing her leg higher, her heat closer.

When he had her leg where he wanted it, he scooped the other leg up, lifting her with an ease that belied her height and weight. She wasn't petite. But he held her.

Her ankles locked behind his back as his palms found the rounded cheeks of her behind and dug in. As if she weighed nothing, he swung her around, catching her mouth with his again while walking them into the bedroom.

Mina was now grateful for the enormous bed

that had seemed too much when she'd entered the room earlier. As it was, it took too long for him to reach it, where he laid her down, his eyes taking her in like a pillaging conqueror.

It wasn't hard to picture him that way. Her very own dark warrior with piercing violet eyes. His body was perfection personified—that of a man who obviously believed in hard work—a wall of well-defined muscles all the way down.

There was finally nothing left to the imagination, and for that Mina was intensely grateful. Her imagination had been woefully inadequate when compared to the real thing. The trail of fine hair began at his navel expanded into a wider, thicker plateau from which a manhood jutted that put every diagram and model she'd ever seen to shame.

Looking at him, her heart pounding, she began to truly understand that the urge to join was about far more than basic biology. It wasn't biology that had her lips parting, that filled her with the boldness to meet his eyes as she let her legs fall open, not hiding any part of herself from him.

He rewarded her action by devouring her with his eyes, the heat of their caress as physical as if it were his body leaning down to cover her. He brought his palms down to the bed, his arms bracketing her on either side of her head, his face above her own before he once again claimed her lips.

She pressed into his kiss, returning it with everything she had, their tongues dancing with one another. His hardness pressed hotly against her core, its temperature somehow registering despite her internal inferno, and she wiggled her hips towards his, instinctively seeking the angle that would bring them even closer together.

Smiling into their kiss, he said, "Patience, Mina *amora*. I want to savor you."

His words danced across her bare skin, leaving shivers in their wake. Bringing her arms up to wrap them around him, she traced patterns on his back with a light scratch of her nails, reveling in the unbridled access to the broad expanse of skin.

For this night, the King—no, Zayn—was hers and hers alone, and she didn't have to worry about whether she was Dr. Aldaba or Queen Amina. Here he was Zayn and she was Mina—a man and a woman in a dance as old as time.

Leaning close, he set a trail of light kisses at her jaw, then travelled down her neck and along her collarbone, along the outside edges of her breasts and down her ribs beneath, before circling around to find her nipple once again.

She arched her back to meet him, moaning as the heat of his mouth enveloped the tender tip.

Then he was pressing his lips against her sternum, and lower, in a path that would soon intersect with her navel and beyond.

A tremor shook her body when his lips reached the upper edge of the patch of hair at the junction of her thighs. Rather than continue in a straight path from there, as she'd expected, he took a detour, tracing feather-light electric kisses teasingly along the edges and her inner thighs. Her skin tightened, pulling taut with each press of his lips, her breath catching every time he exhaled against her skin.

Her hips lifted of their own accord, inner heat building as each breath was hitched, caught and released, no match for his sensory onslaught.

When his lips finally pressed against the seam that held her together she cried out with relief, the thrumming anticipation reaching a fever-pitch she knew would break her apart.

He explored her with gentle strokes of his tongue, slowly delving deeper into her core, traversing ground no man had ever walked before with an intimacy that should have left her shaking with nerves but instead threatened to undo her with pleasure. It rolled through her in waves, each one closer, tighter, more intense than the last. Moans escaped her lips with growing urgency, though what was so urgent she didn't know.

"Let me take you, Mina."

The hum of his words against her most intimate center pushed her over the edge. Shockwaves of sensation ravaged her system. She was arching her back as every muscle in her body tightened then released, leaving her to collapse into a tumbling shell against the bed, her mind dissolved.

But he wasn't done with her yet.

Kissing his way back up, he made quick progress until he once again hovered above her.

"Bend your knees and lift your hips."

The command was absolute. A king's will to be obeyed. And she didn't know if it was due to shock or desire, but she obliged him immediately and shamelessly. His groan at her acquiescence was almost reward enough for her obedience. Almost.

And then he positioned himself at the gateway of her slick entrance and paused, drawing every ounce of her attention to the hot, pulsing point where their bodies touched. She gasped and he grinned rakishly, twitching the head of his shaft against her, teasing her with each flickering movement.

Leaning down, he kissed the hollow behind her ear tracing his lips down along her jaw, whispering as he went. "Do you like the way that feels, Mina?"

She answered with a moan, her body tensing, anticipation building once more. Again her hips wiggled toward him of their own accord, in an instinctive motion urging him to finish what they'd started.

Leaning slightly to one side, he freed his arm to wrap it around Mina's hips, holding her steady as he angled his body and pressed gently against the smoldering heat of her. Her breath caught, her attention zeroing in on the pressure of his hardness, stretching her open, and then he pulled her body closer, catching her mouth in a deep kiss, setting off a sensual onslaught on another front and overwhelming her ability to focus on any single sensation rising inside her.

He entered her slowly, pausing for her slick body to move past the sharp sting of his presence before he pressed deeper, inch by inch, his pace deliciously teasing, luring her to lift her hips and meet his as she stretched to accommodate him.

The thick pressure of him inside her was a wholly new experience, his heat a pulsing rod, radiating warmth from her core outward. Her heart beat in time with its pulse, and the rhythms of their bodies connecting and syncing threatened to dance her into oblivion once again.

She gasped his name and he increased his pace, sliding deeper and deeper into her with each stroke. The veins in his neck and arms were pressing taut against his skin, his own breathing becoming choppy and irregular.

Sensing he was nearing the same peak, she

locked her ankles around his back, angling her hips to allow him even deeper access, driven by primal instruction. He growled in response and the sound sent a wild thrill of possessiveness through her. Tightening her arms around his back, she dug her nails into him, marking him as hers even as he irrevocably claimed her body with each thrust.

"*Ay, Dio*, Mina!"

The words were ripped free from his lips, their strained tenor nudging her own system ever closer toward the edge they both teetered on. They moved in sync, drawn together by a kind of magnetism that had nothing to do with poles, their breath coming fast, their bodies slick with sweat.

A jumbled assortment of words rose in her mind and slipped between her parted lips. "Yes. Keep going. Don't stop."

He obliged, maintaining a pace that was driving her crazy with no sign of flagging, his endurance and stamina obviously a match for the demands of her body.

And demanding it was. Inexperience seemed to have no effect on its sense of entitlement to the pleasure she knew only he could provide. The bonds that held them together made this her right and, overtaken as she was by the sensations it set off, she had every intention of exercising it.

"Mina, Mina, Mina..." Her name was a chanted prayer on his lips, a desperate litany dancing torturously along her nerve-endings, each utterance a lick of fire.

Tension screwed his body tight and he sped up, no longer holding back the force of his own need. She felt the edge of his control in every cell of her body, its rigid urgency weaving them even closer together, binding them toward a fall that would obliterate them both.

"Zayn..." His name on her lips was its own form of begging—a plea for him to carry them into oblivion together.

He obliged, surging into her, plunging them both over the edge, until they dissolved into twin waves, each pulsing deep inside as he emptied himself into her, every heated jet shattering them both into millions of little pieces.

Undone, Mina fell back into the plush mattress she had only just noticed. Zayn dropped to his elbows, his arms still bracketing her, his body hovering just above hers.

A laugh bubbled out of her. She doubted laughing was standard pillow-talk, but the sound had escaped before she'd had the presence to be self-conscious enough to stop it. And it felt good.

Still smiling, she looked up at him and said, "You can relax. You're not going to crush me."

Something like hope flashed across his gaze

before he bent down to catch her lips with his. This kiss wasn't the passionate demand of his earlier kisses. Instead it was a soft command, infused with warmth, that wrapped around her from the inside out and held her there.

When he pulled away, though, anything she thought she'd seen was gone, replaced by the charm of the practiced grin he flashed at her before collapsing on her dramatically. He rolled off quickly, then reached for her again as they settled side by side.

Still wondering at that look she'd seen in his eyes, she nestled closer to him, for the first time in her life unwilling to ask a question and risk breaking a moment in the name of curiosity.

Hints of that strange warmth were creeping back into her skin, and now that she'd seen where following sensation could lead, she wanted to follow where these took her as well.

"Are you sore?" Zayn asked.

The question had her cheeks heating, even after the experience they'd just shared. "I'm comfortable, thank you," she said, her voice taking on a prim note she couldn't seem to hold back.

Holding her as he was, she felt his low chuckle ripple through his entire frame. "It's a reasonable thing to ask after a woman's first time."

Mina's body flushed a hot red. "Who's to say it was my first time?"

Laughing, he pulled her closer. "I am, Mina *amora*."

"Hymen lore is mostly that—lore," she said tartly.

"I don't claim any expertise in the mythology," he said, then paused before continuing in a dry voice, "But I felt yours."

"Oh." Well, she had *tried* to save her dignity.

After a long pause, he asked, "Are you embarrassed?" His voice held surprise.

Mina opened her mouth to deny it, but the automatic response seemed foolish, given the circumstances. Instead, she said, "A little. At a certain point virginity becomes a bit sad."

He shook his head. "No. It's not. You were dedicated to something bigger."

Something raw and jagged inside her began to knit itself together at his words, and while she wanted to think it was the result of being validated by someone other than her parents after all these years, she had a feeling it had everything to do with who was doing the validating.

Rolling over in his arms, she faced him, her head tilted to take him in. As always, his eyes locked on hers when given the opportunity, violet latching onto hazel like a missile on target. And, as always, the contact struck her, holding her frozen and breathless in its possession.

His expression lit with knowing as he held her,

a naughty grin lifting the corner of his mouth as he squeezed her. "I like it. All mine."

His voice carried a note of surprise, as if he hadn't expected the truth of his own words, and she got the distinct impression that while it might not have been something he'd ever thought about before, he meant it now.

That realization came with its own thrill, and this time it was she who instigated their kiss, scooting up close to gently press her lips to his. He drew her tighter against his body and returned the kiss. Then, pulling them both more fully onto the bed, he turned her over so her back fit snugly against his chest, her rear end was tucked into the juncture of his hips, his arms wrapped around her.

Once they were settled, he turned the lights down and pressed a final kiss against the back of her neck. Quietly, he said, "Goodnight, Mina."

"Goodnight, Zayn," she whispered back, reveling in the feel of him all around her, on her lips, at her back, and deep in her core.

CHAPTER EIGHT

IT WASN'T THE light that woke him—not with the thick curtains that covered the windows. Neither was it a discreet knock from a member of staff. There was no staff here at the cabin. No. It was the lush weight of warm breasts resting on his forearm, the rounded curves of female anatomy pressed tight against him, and the long shapely legs intertwined with his own that transitioned him from dreams into even more pleasant reality.

He couldn't remember the last time he'd woken up with a woman. Not since he'd been crowned. He had been with women, of course, but it just didn't do for a parade of women to creep in and out of the King's bedroom. His assignations were discreet, taking place in secret locations, and were more likely to include a nondisclosure agreement than a morning-after.

To make matters more unfamiliar, in this case it wasn't merely waking up together. It was having had breakfast and dinner together the previous day. It was a feeling of true relaxation and peace that, while he'd like to chalk it up to the location, he knew had to do with the company. It was a merging of bodies that had reached inside him and stirred things up, rearranging him from the inside out without his permission or regard. It was all that and more. And with his wife of all people.

It wasn't safe. If he'd learned anything from his parents' example it was that. Regardless of what his father had believed, a king must never allow anything to come between him and his country. Not even his wife. Especially not his wife. They'd all seen what could happen in the aftermath of that.

And so he didn't stay where he was, content in a way he couldn't remember being since he'd truly understood what it meant to be the heir to the throne, nestled happily with a woman he was bound by law to love and cherish. Instead, he eased his arm free from under her neck and head, unwound his legs, and slowly pulled away from her.

She murmured in protest, but didn't wake— not that he'd expected her to...the previous day had been enough to tax an elite soldier—and, even though he was tempted to return, to pull her close and place gentle kisses along the back of her neck until she heated and stirred, willing and ready to greet the day with him in brand-new ways, he resisted the urge. He forced himself to step away from the siren draw of the woman on the bed and search instead for the clean pants he'd discarded the night before.

Tearing his mind from her, he forced it toward the morning. They should leave the cabin immediately. Breakfast together would be far too intimate an affair after the night they'd shared. If they prepared food and sat down across from each other again at that small table, just the two of them, he knew that the deep ease that existed between them would be ever-present, even in the face of what would be her inevitable new shyness.

She was his now, in a way she was no other man's, now or ever.

The thought was more satisfying than it should be.

No, breakfast at the cabin would definitely be a bad idea. And if he felt a twinge of guilt at evading eating with her, he vowed to make up for it by ensuring she had a wonderful time on the island—including the full spa experience. But she would need something in her system before they set out on their short hike to the summer palace, and since she had made dinner, and he was in the mood to dote on her, he decided to put together a small bite to eat.

Satisfied with the plan, he executed it, putting

the kettle on for Mina's tea before tossing two croissants in the toaster. He then cut two thick slices of deli ham, a peach and some strawberries, before grabbing some soft white cheese from a plate in the refrigerator. Now all he had to do was make a cup of coffee and wait for Mina.

Twenty minutes later she came into the kitchen, quietly but without timidity, and he was impressed. He imagined her steeling herself, squaring her shoulders in that way that was becoming familiar, before walking into his sight. The corner of his lip lifted. Her hair was pulled into a high curly ponytail and she wore clothing that fit her for once, fresh hiking gear that consisted of purple leggings that hugged her hips and long legs paired with a snug fitted windbreaker in light gray.

"There's tea," he said, nodding toward the mug that rested on the counter as she neared. He'd noticed at breakfast the day before that she had taken tea over coffee, with two sugars and cream.

"Oh, thank you, that sounds heavenly." The warmth of genuine pleasure filled her voice at the news, and he was glad that he'd gone ahead and prepared the tea for her, rather than wait to ask when she came down.

She took a big sip and moaned with delight and he couldn't help but smile again—both at her hedonistic enjoyment and her ability to gulp down the steaming hot beverage without regard for the temperature.

"I see where my real value lies in this marriage," he said.

The word "marriage" must have reminded her of the night they'd shared, because her cheeks darkened, and a dusky rose tint overlaid her golden-brown skin.

"Oh, well. Good, then…" she stuttered lightly, obviously flustered by the images flashing across her mind.

He wondered what she saw. Was it him? Was it their bodies coming together, joining in the most primal way?

Picturing her mind filled with images of their lovemaking set his own body off, his blood heating as he too recalled losing himself in her, the complete release of everything, if only momentarily—even the fact that he was King.

That last thought was enough to shake the spell.

Stepping back, he said, "We'll have a real brunch at the summer palace. After that massages, soaking pools, salt wraps, and another massage. Think of our time here as the spa trip you missed out on."

Mina's eyes had lit up at the word "massages," and he was glad that he'd made the decision. They would spend the next few days together, enjoying the island and each other, free to explore the exquisite fit of their bodies as much as the island's beaches. And while they were doing all that he wouldn't need to examine why he felt at peace for the first time since his father's death.

He watched Mina finish her light breakfast, making small talk while eating himself. Once finished, he washed the dishes, as was his custom at the cabin, and they readied themselves to leave.

"The trail from here to the summer palace is a reasonable distance, but it's easy hiking the whole way, and doesn't take long. Its long enough to feel like you've accomplished something, but not so far it's a strain."

She grinned. "What are we waiting for? Massages are at the other end!"

And then she took off, without a backward glance. And just like that she made something as commonplace as a massage brand-new and exciting again.

Zayn followed briskly, eager for a change in scenery, though all he seemed to have eyes for was the woman in front of him.

"The summer palace is beautiful."

The words were out before he'd thought about them, an unconscious attempt to solicit one of her golden smiles.

She turned to him, a spark of interest brightening her eye. "I can't wait to see it. D'Tierrza said you spent a lot of time there, growing up?"

He nodded, remembering those days of running wild at the summer palace hiding away from the public eye. "I did. It gave us a chance to be normal."

Mina surprised him by laughing. "Normal children don't have private islands—but I understand what you mean. As normal as possible for a prince."

He smiled, giving in to the urge to touch her, caressing the back of the hand nearest him with a finger as he said, "You don't have much sympathy for your Prince."

Her cheeks darkened, but she didn't move her hand. "It's not good to be too sympathetic toward powerful people—it inflates their egos."

Not bothering to fight the wicked spark her words lit in him, he leaned closer, his lips near her ear and his voice low as he said, "It's so good for me that I have you to take care of my...ego."

Before his eyes, the slight darkening of Mina's cheeks blossomed into a full-bodied blush. As close as they stood, he could feel the heat radiating from her body. He was leaning in to take her lips before he knew what he was doing, capturing their plump fullness before the warning to keep her at a distance could go off.

She leaned into him without hesitation, opening her mouth to what was becoming the familiar dance of their lips meeting.

He took what she offered without hesitation, reveling in the sensation of freedom she brought him: freedom to take, freedom to plunder his sweet prize without regard for propriety and decorum, freedom to unleash the force of his unvarnished personality and know that she not only had the full capacity to handle it, but would meet him with her own passion and intensity.

She returned his kiss with a new boldness. Her body was coming to understand the power it held over him even if her mind, new to the back and forth between a man and a woman, had yet to grasp it.

She made him forget himself each and every time, over and over, and he had the distinct impression that the experience would only continue—no matter how many times he came to the well, he would leave thirsting for more. She was dangerous, but he didn't pull away from their kiss. He couldn't.

When he did finally pull back, he looked at her, beautiful green eyes still closed, her face glowing and bright, and he locked the image tight in his mind, storing it.

She opened her eyes then, and they glittered like polished gems. He couldn't look away...entranced like a dragon with its hoard.

* * *

Less than an hour later they once again left the forest to enter a clearing—this one even more massive than the last. It opened into a large secluded bay, with a gorgeous dark brown sandy beach, arched cliffs, and there, like a bright white beacon, standing proud and timeless, was the summer palace.

Dashing into the clearing to take in the stunning structure, Mina gasped loudly.

Her reaction brought a smile to his face. The summer palace had that effect on people.

His ancestors had had a thing for white marble, and it showed nowhere more than here at the summer palace. Embedded into the landscape, the building incorporated both the forested hill and the natural cliffside, with thick rounded columns, open-air patios, and breathtaking views all the way around. Inside, the palace was completely modernized, boasting every convenience and then some, and was powered entirely by renewable energy.

She was going to love it here—he knew it. It was impossible not to.

Palace staff greeted them at the stairs, and he quickly reassured them of their health and safety, as well as calling for brunch. They had both worked up an appetite after their morning hike.

Like everything at the summer palace, brunch

was both elaborate and relaxed. Spread across a long table, the menu included island classics—olives, fresh cheese, bread, and pâté—as well as delicious flavors from farther afield, like coconut pudding, *kheer*, fresh mango, pineapple, and starfruit.

Eyeing the food, Mina sat regally in the chair that had been pulled out for her, though he was sure she didn't realize it. He doubted that she would believe anything she did was regal.

A frown came to his face at the thought. Her self-doubt was, in part, his fault. Which was unfortunate. Freed from her academic disguise, she was truly lovely. Her mind was exacting, and yet she was humble. She had withstood shock, devastation and, if he were being honest, mild humiliation with grace and those squared shoulders of hers. If only she had the ability to hide everything she was feeling, she might have the makings of an excellent queen.

They dined al fresco, on a patio overlooking the island's small bay, falling into what was quickly becoming a pattern of easy conversation.

"That water in the bay looks divine," she said, and sighed, closing her eyes.

He smiled. "It's warm, too."

"I'm definitely swimming. Or not…" Words that had started high ended low.

"Why not?"

"My swimsuit is back at the plane."

Zayn shook his head, laughing. "There's probably a selection for you to choose from in your closet."

It only took her a moment to recover from being taken aback this time. A sign she was adjusting to royal life. That was good.

"It's odd to think of it as being mine."

She still needed to work on that earnest forthrightness, though. Otherwise, sooner or later, she'd be skewered. The thought irritated him.

"Well, I'm sure it will sink in eventually."

The words came out sharper than he'd intended, but she merely glanced at him before turning back to the view, and he was glad. Let her focus on relaxing. She didn't need to know she was tying him up in knots.

CHAPTER NINE

BY THE END of her massage she was a human puddle in all the best ways possible. Each and every muscle in her body had been seen to, and after the dancing, the emergency landing, the hiking, and...other things, each and every muscle in her body had *needed* seeing to.

She was beginning to see a pattern in Zayn's communication with her. He might be presumptuous and autocratic, but he was tender and thoughtful at the same time. Relaxed and pleased, she asked staff to direct her to their rooms.

Not finding him there, she detoured, exploring the closet prepared for her by the summer palace staff. They'd provided a selection of items for her for every possible island activity she could imagine. Spying the tasteful lingerie among the neatly stored clothing, she added emphasis to the word *every*.

For the moment, she thought, she wanted to feel comfortable, but also...*pretty*. Instead of shoving the urge away, she let herself wish for them—for the frivolous things she'd shunned for so long. She wanted to look pretty when Zayn saw her.

And, as if her life had truly turned into a fairy tale, she found what she was looking for in a cashmere lounging set, with an off-the-shoulder top and silk ribbon drawstring pants in a rich, creamy ivory color. The slippers she found were decadently soft, each step a mini foot-rub.

Successfully finding clothing that was both comfortable and pretty, in her own closet, had to be one of the more positive novelties of her new life. And, taking in her reflection in the full-length mirror, she had to admit to herself it definitely had a confidence-boosting effect that was almost magical.

Feeling as soft and decadent outside as she felt inside, she looked for Zayn in his office next, locating it after one wrong turn and a second request for directions, only to find it empty.

She didn't find him in any of the spas, theaters, lounges, libraries, gardens, or patios she checked either. It was only when she stood with her hands on her hips in the foyer, at her wits' end as yet another idea turned up with a gorgeous room but no sign of her husband, that a maid stepped forward quietly and tapped her shoulder.

"If you're looking for His Majesty, Your Majesty, you won't find him here. He's down on the beach."

"Thank you," Mina said to the woman, before heading down to find him.

Beside the front door was an assortment of styles of sandals. She chose a simple thong sandal before making her way to the beach. There she found a small blanket and towel laid out, but no sign of the King.

Scanning a horizon that was growing ever more golden with each passing hour, with her hand held up to shield her eyes from the glare of the sun off the sea, she saw him only when he crested the waves in a powerful butterfly stroke, the sunlight glinting off the bright tan of his broad shoulders, which were balanced with perfect strength and symmetry. His whole body looked weightless for a heartbeat, before he disappeared once more beneath the water.

He was as perfect and natural at sea as he was on land. She wondered if there was any landscape he wasn't the master of. He certainly never seemed to lose his footing. Perhaps that came with being born a future king.

Taking a seat on his blanket, she was content to watch him as he swam, his body appearing and disappearing in the surf, which crashed with soothing power and rhythm. On the beach, with the waves lulling her heart, perfectly safe here on a private island—as improbable as that was—watching her gorgeous husband swim, she let go of the last of the grief for her broken dreams.

She had achieved everything she'd set out to do. Not many people could say that. And if the triumph hadn't lasted as long as she had imagined it would, she was not so lacking in gratitude that she couldn't be thankful that this was where she had landed after the fall.

There were a lot worse things to be than Queen.

Zayn joined her on the beach not long after, his chiseled body dripping with seawater. As suspected, the reality of it was a thousand times more seductive than the vision her imagination had conjured in the bath the night before.

Staring up at him boldly as he dried fanned the seemingly ever-present flame that existed for him at her core. He watched her just as boldly, noting her every reaction with his amethyst gaze, unhurried by her regard, and when he was satisfied he sat beside her on the blanket, looking out to sea.

"Good swim?" she asked.

"Wonderful. I had forgotten how well the water clears the mind. It's been too long since I've come here."

"When was the last time?"

"Just after graduation. I spent an entire week here with my father and mother. We jet-skied, hiked, spent a night at the cabin, played charades…"

He reminisced quietly as they watched the pink beginnings of the sunset.

She laughed. "It's hard to imagine you playing charades. Or your mother, for that matter."

"But you can picture my father?" he asked, with mock outrage.

Mina nodded. "He had that certain something."

Flat-voiced, Zayn said, "Don't say he was approachable."

"Well, he was..." she hedged.

Zayn growled, and she held up her hands in surrender, giggling.

"He was! But it was more than that. There was something about King Alden that made him seem like he was just like the rest of us. A regular person."

Zayn snorted. "That was just the image he wanted to project. He was a king, through and through."

"You miss him," she said.

He looked away from her then, his eyes going again to the sea. "Every day."

"You were close?"

"Very. We discussed everything—philosophy, economics, justice, rule. He shaped me, even when we didn't agree."

She smiled. "My father was the same. Though he and I were always in agreement. Or at least I always agreed with him," she amended.

"My father sometimes encouraged disagreement, though it was rare."

Intrigued, she asked, "What did you disagree about?"

He looked at her then, considering her before he said, "Love."

"Oh, really? What thoughts did the man who betrothed his son before his birth have on love?" she asked archly.

A lopsided smile tilted Zayn's face. "Believe me, I've asked myself that question a number of times over the past months," he said.

The light chuckle he added took the sting out of the statement. They were no longer adversaries, Mina thought, but in this together. Somewhere in the past two days they'd gone from being two strangers to a team.

"No. Ironically, he insisted that my top priority be falling in love—the very health of the nation depended on it, he said."

Mina frowned. "And you don't agree?" she asked.

He shook his head, not catching her shadowed expression. "I think the nation benefits most from a skilled monarch who brings something of value to the crown."

Keeping her voice light, Mina asked, "And what do I bring to the crown?"

"Initially, I wasn't sure," he said frankly, "but

then you took care of me during our hike, so it's obvious you were destined to bring ease to the crown."

He spoke loftily, his nose in the air high enough to ensure she knew he was teasing, and she had another glimpse of the man he'd been before tragedy had replaced his carefree life with rock-steady rule.

Drily, she replied, "I'm so glad I can bring so much value to the crown."

Laughing, he wrapped an arm around her shoulders and pulled her to him. "You keep surprising me with your hidden talents. I'm sure I will never know the limits of your value."

Cheeks now aflame, she didn't know what to say. His smile turning wicked, he leaned closer, and she somehow knew that if he kissed her then—if his lips touched hers while her heart was still stuttering from his words—something terrible would happen…something that would change her forever.

Her mind grasped for the first thing it could, to put space between them before he closed the distance. And because, no matter how her life changed, she couldn't change who she was, what came out was about his work.

"So, tell me about the Ambassadors' Dinner?"

The blurted-out question was enough to halt

him for the moment, but rather than look irritated by her evasion, he let his smile turn arrogant.

Leaning back, he said, "This dinner is particularly important for securing a diplomatic relationship with the Farden, a small German-speaking country with excellent mineral resources. This is their first visit to the island and we want them to see that we are sophisticated and modern—that establishing ties with us is not a risk to their reputation. As members of one of the few remaining constitutional monarchies of Europe, you and I represent both our entire nation and an outdated, increasingly unfavored form of rule. As such, it is crucial we convey progressive thought and current awareness."

Mina nodded, finding herself intrigued by the concept of strategizing an event appearance. "That all makes sense."

"My goal is a verbal commitment from the Chancellor that we will formalize a diplomatic relationship between our two countries by the end of dinner. Conversation will be in English throughout the evening, which makes it a great relief to find that you speak it so well."

Mina smiled, warming under his praise. She spoke German like a natural-born citizen as well, having learned in the cradle and spent summers there with her grandparents before her studies began to tether her to her desk, but didn't mention it for fear of looking like she was fishing for praise.

Unaware of her private bashfulness, Zayn continued, "We've secured relationships with England, Sweden, France, Italy, Spain, Australia, New Zealand, Ireland and Greece already, so I have no doubt we can do so with Farden as well."

Mina agreed. "I don't see why you wouldn't. Cyrano shows all the signs of being Europe's next 'undiscovered gem.' It would be in their interest to smooth the way for their citizens to take advantage."

Zayn leaned forward, his eyes lighting, "My thinking exactly. And Cyrano will benefit because the relationship will serve as an example of exactly the kind we need to ensure that it truly becomes just that."

She laughed. "That's a rather calculated game of chicken and egg."

He smiled, his expression wide, open, and genuine. "Not an incorrect description of statecraft."

They continued their conversation on the beach, strategizing on how they would approach the Ambassadors' Dinner, until the beginning chill of the evening and hunger sent them inside.

That night they dined on exquisitely prepared fresh seafood, and then made love in the summer palace's stunning master suite until neither could breathe.

* * *

The next three days continued in much the same fashion: hiking, swimming, bird-watching, dining al fresco and, of course, having massages. All too soon, though, it was time to return to the real world—and, more importantly, the Ambassadors' Dinner.

Their plane was due within the hour.

Mina's attire for the dinner would be waiting on her arrival in the Queen's Wing, along with Roz and the entire team, ready to prepare her yet again for the state function. Mina had made it clear following the ball that, while she wanted none of them to feel beholden to her, she would welcome each and every one of them to her permanent team. They had all accepted.

It was good to be Queen.

The King's guards, as well as Moustafa and d'Tierrza, met them at the private airport. Zayn nodded to his guards, who fell into their usual positions around him. Mina greeted her own guards with a smile that was bright and beaming and pulled each one into a hug. Moustafa stiffened, but quickly relaxed into the embrace. D'Tierrza returned it with strong-armed enthusiasm.

Zayn said goodbye to her when they reached the palace. "I need to check in with my assistant before dinner. I'll see you tonight." He bowed slightly to her, kissing her temple before leaving.

Mina, Moustafa, and d'Tierrza met Roz's team in the Queen's Wing.

"What happened to you?" Roz rasped.

Mina laughed. "Too much to recount—and we covered what's important when we spoke on the phone. Tonight it is imperative that I project the correct image—as well as the extra part I mentioned."

Roz nodded, a wicked light brightening her countenance. "Right. Cool, modern, and bringing the King to his knees within the appropriate limits of a state dinner."

"Exactly!" A little thrill trilled through Mina's blood.

The team got to work. Chloe, Roz's assistant, as usual all in black, ran errands for the rest of the team—fetching a brush for Byron, the hairstylist, an eyeshadow for Sabine, the aesthetician with the perfect face, and pins for Catriona, the designer with the asymmetrical haircut.

When they were done, Mina was once again transformed. This time she was all sharp edges and shadows. Her hair had been pulled back into a sleek and elegant French twist, without a wisp out of place, and she wore a custom-fitted black one-piece pantsuit.

Deep V cutouts adorned the chest and back of the suit, with panels of sheer fabric in dark black sewn in for modesty. The design displayed the distinct impression of the curves of her breasts without showcasing any actual cleavage. The sleeves were fitted and full-length, tapering to narrow slightly at the wrists. Everything she wore followed and hugged the lines of her body—no one would dare call this suit boxy.

Roz had chosen diamonds as her only accessory—enormous teardrops at her earlobes and a monstrous solitaire hanging on a long platinum chain in the center of her breasts.

For shoes, they'd selected simple black leather pumps with heels high enough to add a few more inches to her legs. Once again the heels had bright red soles and a foreign name tastefully stamped into the leather.

Sabrina had made her eyes look smoky and large, without being overly dark and dramatic, and used a muted dusky rose for her lips, ensuring she looked alluring, yet professional.

Dressed in all black, she would be the perfect complement to Zayn, ensuring that they presented an image of sleek, young and modern monarchs, just as he wanted. She would be everything he said a queen ought to be: temptation in an untouchable package—at least not until long after the dinner was over.

His face when she met him in the foyer justified the effort. His gaze heated, igniting an answering flame in her that she let him see, but she kept tortuously outside of his arm's reach. He wore a black suit with a black button-up shirt and tie.

"You look lovely. Excellent choice for the evening."

She smiled at his compliment. Roz had taught her an important lesson—one she had already subconsciously observed in academia: clothes made the man—or the woman, the professor, or the Queen. Tonight she had dressed the part. Together they were a pair of silk-clad ravens, grave and imposing. And the sporadic flares of electricity between them only emphasized the intense magnetism that paired them.

Mina inclined her head with a cool, "Thank you."

He led the way to the entrance, where their driver held open the limo door. Mina thanked the man as she entered the vehicle, and slid along the smooth leather seats to sit beside the window. Zayn followed her into the car and the driver shut the door.

They arrived at the venue to find a red carpet and flashing cameras. Cyrano was certainly developing a celebrity culture—paparazzi and press included.

Zayn slid an arm around her waist, the heat of the contact branding her through the layers of fabric that separated them, and he smiled, obliging the media covering their arrival and sending a thrill down her spine at the same time.

He was an excellent multitasker.

The dinner was being held in the grand ballroom of the Palace Museum—an aristocratic palace in the capital that had fallen out of the hands of its original owners nearly a century before and had been purchased by a private citizen and art collector. Upon his death, the palace and the collection it housed had been converted into a museum.

Mina had been to private events at the Palace Museum throughout her academic career, but nothing as grand as the occasion before her now. The museum had clearly spared no expense for the evening, and every effort had been made to impress the distinguished guests, which included all of Cyrano's standing ambassadors and their families, in addition to other delegates from the nations Cyrano was courting relationships with, as well as members of Parliament and the bulk of the island's aristocrats.

As they approached the Chancellor Klein, Mina's nerves around the importance of the encounter, coupled with the constant exertion of withstanding her inconveniently relentless attraction to her husband, had her pulled taut as a bowstring. Practiced smile in place, however,

she vowed to herself that she would do nothing
to jeopardize the relationship Zayn sought.

In fact, filled with an oddly protective determination, Mina reached for Zayn's hand and
squeezed it as they walked, unthinkingly mir-
roring the reassurance her father had used to give
her before every big event.

The memory flashed through her without any
of the acrid tang that memories of her father had
recently taken on, and she was glad, hoping that
it meant the process of forgiveness had begun.
She might never be able to think of him in quite
the same way again, but their love had been real.
His peerless rooting for her had been real.

She didn't understand why he'd done it, but she
could accept that her father had arranged the betrothal out of love. And somehow, as if acknowledging that had shattered the shield of ignorance
that had been protecting her, as her hand clasped
his, she realized that she loved Zayn.

Not in the enduring and mellow way she loved
her mother, and not in the vague, patriotic way
she loved Cyrano. It wasn't the complicated,
angry, nostalgic, yearning love for her father either, and it wasn't her captivating love of study.

She loved him the way a woman loved a man.

Passionate, greedy, and demanding. Intense,
delicate, and needy. She loved him for trying to
make her strong enough for the job at the same

time as trying to make up for everything becoming royalty had changed in her life. She loved him with her full self. And so, for the first time, she felt engaged—fully and completely—with everyday life. She was no longer preparing for the future or breaking over the past. She was here, in the present moment, absolutely in love.

And it was time to meet the Chancellor.

The Chancellor, a slender gray-haired woman with impeccable style and wireless glasses, wore a graphite pantsuit and sensible black pumps. Her husband was on a well-televised reconciliation tour of the African continent, so she had brought her college-aged son Werner to attend the dinner with her instead. The two of them stood with a number of other Farden officials who had made the trip alongside the family.

Chancellor Klein's son's interest in politics was well known, and he was expected to make a bid to turn his family into Farden's first political dynasty within the next decade. Already famous in his own right, the striking blond youth also happened to be athletic and highly intelligent, on his way to graduating with honors from Cambridge. Werner was the kind of star pupil Mina had seen pass through her classroom only rarely, as they typically bypassed Cyrano's humble Capital University to travel to more internationally renowned institutions.

Mina smiled warmly as she and Zayn closed the distance between themselves and the foreign visitors, first catching Chancellor Klein's savvy blue eyes before turning her gaze slightly to include her son.

As their eyes connected the young man's expression took on a glint Mina did not immediately recognize, both haughty and hungry at the same time, and she schooled her features so as not to give away her confusion as she allowed him to take her hand. He bent over it with a kiss and a smile while Zayn engaged with his mother.

In English, he said, "I had heard the Queen of Cyrano was a common woman of rare beauty, but the reports do not do you justice."

Rather than feeling flattered, she realized his words had set off an unpleasant sensation, crawling along the outer edges of her skin.

"You're very kind, Mr. Klein. It's lovely to have you and your esteemed mother here in our beloved Cyrano."

"And it is lovely to be here. Cyranese hospitality lives up to its legend."

She had no idea why, but although his words were innocent, Mina felt the urge to use hand sanitizer after he'd said them.

Obviously catching the tail-end of Werner's sentence as he turned from the Chancellor, Zayn said, "I am glad to hear that. We're here to serve.

Let our staff know what you would like, and we'll do everything we can to accommodate you."

Having made their introductions and initial contact, Zayn and Mina had turned to make their way to the dining room when Werner Klein leaned toward one of his companions with a chuckle and said, in distinctly audible German, "I'd like to see if his wife could accommodate *me.*"

Mina sucked in a quiet breath. At her side, Zayn was suddenly all rapid motion and purpose, closing the short distance they'd walked away from the younger Klein in seconds, to return to his side.

The sudden movement of the King caused a ripple of awareness to go through the crowd, drawing conversations to a halt and bringing all of the attention in the room to him—just in time to witness the precise cocking back of his elbow and the jackhammering of his fist directly into Werner's face.

One. Two. Three. And Werner collapsed on the ground.

Color draining from her face, the Chancellor took a step toward her son but then seemed to hesitate, unwilling to approach the darkly radiating monarch.

Dressed in black, and towering over the unconscious man, Zayn looked every inch the me-

dieval warrior King, despite the modern lines of
his suit and his insistence that Cyrano had moved
past its history.

Werner's cronies stepped closer, gaining confidence after their friend's embarrassment. In moments, there would be an all-out brawl.

Watching as Zayn's plans crumbled around
him, Mina felt something click inside her. Dr.
Aldaba might never have been caught dead in her
current outfit—too distracting, after all—but the
impenetrable professor and scientist was as much
a part of her bones as Queen Amina.

She squared her shoulders and crossed the
space between her and the two men as if she
was strolling across her lecture room rather than
a ballroom at a grand event.

She placed cool fingertips on the King's elbow
and he stilled, the radiating physicality of his intent toward the younger man dimming. And as
she restrained him she also said in soft, smooth,
and rapid German, her tone at once censuring
and commanding—the same tone her mother had
used on her to calm her rare tantrums as a child,
"Gentlemen. I don't believe it is considered po-
lite to scuffle indoors. I'm going to have to insist
you take this outdoors."

Zayn shot her a glance that she knew had more
to do with the fact that she'd held back her lan-

guage abilities than the censure in her tone. He did step back, however.

The other men, having been accessories to Werner's original comment, were not handling the revelation of the Queen's language skills nearly so well. Two sets of eyes were glued to Mina in abject horror. She recognized the look of individuals staring career failure in the face, but couldn't muster much empathy. She had been a teacher long enough to recognize a group of entitled rich kids a mile away.

As the threat of physical violence dissipated, the Chancellor stepped inside the circle, her hawk eyes taking in the fact that her son was on the floor and that all his cronies had lost their color.

"What's going on here?" she asked quietly, speaking in German as well.

Mina opened her mouth, ready to answer for all of them, using the tone she had used as a professor to report to a parent on a student's progress, but Zayn's hand on her wrist stopped her.

"I would advise that you leave your son at home next time, Chancellor Klein."

Zayn's voice was a whip through the room and Chancellor Klein's mouth dropped open.

Mina grimaced, adding public rebuking to the list of primeval King's rights that Zayn was exercising tonight. But even though she felt for the woman—it wasn't her fault her son's behavior had been inexcusable—Mina couldn't help but observe, as Zayn dragged her out of the ballroom, that he had been right. The open-mouthed expression really did make one look like a fish.

CHAPTER TEN

ZAYN'S REIN ON his temper was hanging by a thin thread, and he had already taken violent action against the son of a head of state.

"You will never speak of my wife again," he had growled in German, just before hitting the man with the cold clarity and precision his instructors had always told him to seek.

As a man, Zayn had encountered Werner Klein's kind many times, and he knew that the best way to deal with that kind of bully was to smash them like an ant and move on. And he'd done exactly that.

That was not, however, how a king dealt with his problems.

Kings treated men like Klein as gnats—unworthy of notice or reaction.

No. He had not acted like a king. He had acted like a man—and not just a man, but a hot-headed youth, the kind of young man he had been when he had gone away to college, wild and unable to carry the responsibility of the crown, rather than the level-headed monarch he'd schooled himself to be.

And it was all because of Mina.

He had acted more like his father than himself, and that was a luxury he could not afford—not when vipers lay in wait to take advantage of his every weakness.

He had put his woman before the needs of the nation.

The thought bounced around inside him like an angry wasp he could neither force out of his consciousness nor bury beneath his growing fury.

"Slow down, Zayn. I'm new to this height of heel."

Mina's breathless voice finally broke through the storm that was his thoughts. Immediately he slowed, turning to take her in.

Her hair was as controlled as it had been the day they had met, but tonight it elegantly highlighted the sweep of her cheekbones, somehow directing the eye to her lush mouth.

Her mouth was, he knew, an erotic playground, barely charted in the handful of times he'd had the privilege to explore it. And her body, contoured and showcased as it was now, in her one-piece pantsuit, was sexy and untouchable at the same time—a frustrating combination that antagonized the hunger that lived inside him even as it stoked it.

He gave his head a small shake. He was thinking about her too much.

Closing his eyes again, he took a deep breath. He would get them to the car, return to his office once they arrived back at the palace, and immediately begin damage control for the evening. Then he would return to his quarters and go to bed.

A desperate and resolute part of him vowed that it would be alone. Not with her. It couldn't be with her. Not until he had regained his control. It was imperative that he master his reactions to her. The night had made it clear that the issue was no longer merely a personal matter.

In the time they'd been married he'd learned that there was nothing he could focus on that was compelling enough to keep images of her at bay. He was helpless against the flow of erotic flashes of her that danced across his mind the moment his guard was down—and he held the fate of a nation in his hands.

Distance was the only thing that would work. And maybe a drink.

"Zayn!" Mina stomped her foot as she said it, standing on the curb, arms crossed in front of her chest.

He turned his attention to her—or rather the real her. His attention had been unable to focus on anything but her since the moment she'd stepped through the chapel door—with effort.

"What?" His voice held all the cutting chill it had held that long-ago day.

"What's going on?"

She asked the question quietly, delicately walking around the words she didn't say. *What the hell were you thinking? You ruined our plan! Where is your self-control?* And he found that irritated him more than if she'd just gone ahead with recriminations. Lord knew he had earned them.

He hadn't done anything so foolishly scandalous since he had been photographed in Amsterdam years ago, as a university student.

"Zayn?" she said again, with a bit more volume but no less grating delicate concern.

"I hit a man in the face, Mina. And as I am the King, I would think it would be clear what's going on now: I'm trying to determine the correct order of operations to begin immediate damage control."

The car pulled up and their driver jumped out to open the door, wisely sensing that conversation would be neither welcome nor appreciated.

Zayn gestured for Mina to enter the car first before following, his every movement brittle and angry. She opened her mouth, but Zayn stopped her with a hand. "If you are about to offer some meaningless condolence, Mina, I would advise against it."

She closed her mouth, and the ever-growing orb of rage inside of him began to take on a more beastly shape.

It was absolutely absurd that he had actually hit the man—defending his lady's honor like some barbarian of old—and all the more ironic for the fact that he, and his father before him, had spent the bulk of his reign working to separate Cyrano's reputation from its tumultuous feudal past. He had just undone all that with a single action.

"Zayn."

Mina's fingertips pressed lightly at his elbow again. She had scooted closer to him at some point, her perfect body just inches away from his now, and he hadn't noticed. He was deteriorating faster than he'd feared possible.

His entire body stilled.

She leaned closer, placing her palms on either side of his face to draw his gaze to her own. Green and gold swam together, warm and accepting, in a loving promise that it was possible to come back from this. That together it was possible to come back from anything.

And then she was pressing her lips softly against his in a kiss that was feather-light and over before it began. Pulling back, she sparkled an open smile on her face, emanating that same strange sunlight only she seemed to possess.

"It's okay," she said.

She didn't say *I love you*, but she didn't need to. He heard it. And, hearing it, he broke open.

It began as a faint crack in the dam that held back the deep black. His hands thrust out to cup either side of her face, his fingers wrapping around her skull while his thumbs tilted her chin up. His internal structure began to give way as the crack raced across its surface, branching out at rapid speed, freeing the rage of waters held back too long.

Their lips met. Hers were soft and pliant and open, not only willing to absorb the weight and wrongness of his sin, but asking for it, begging him to bury it deep inside her, where she could turn it into something better—something good.

He pulled her into his lap with the force of a wave off the sea. Like so much flotsam, she tumbled into him, ever willing to be swept up in the fierce power of his embrace, open to him whenever he had need. And wasn't that the problem? She was a drug, offered freely, over and over, her only price the abandonment of his honor.

He wanted to push her away.

Instead, he absorbed her.

He demanded her entire focus with his lips, controlled her body, gripping her thighs on either side of him with no intention of allowing her to move, decimating her shields with his will to own and command her entire being.

The car pulled into the palace at some point. He lifted her out, unwilling to break their kiss, and somewhere along his route, carrying her to the Queen's Wing with her legs locked around his waist, the hot core of her scalding even through the fabrics that separated them, he waved off her guards and shooed away the staff.

But he made sure she wasn't aware of any of that. As far as she was concerned, the only thing that existed was him and the sensations he aroused. He would have it no other way. Here, he would be the master and commander. She would experience the feeling of being completely unmoored, completely at the mercy of another human being, her very behavior tethered to whims of another.

He pressed her against the wall in her bedroom, the rigid steel length of him teetering between threat and promise as she leaned into him with force to match his. And then it wasn't enough to press, to be separated by barriers, even those as insubstantial as clothing.

Her carried her to the bed, where he placed her gently on her back before placing his hands on her hips and turning her around until she faced away from him, on her hands and knees. Impatient to have the glorious curves of her at his full disposal, he unzipped her suit and pushed it off her shoulders from behind.

Breathing heavily, she pulled the top half off before he took over, pulling the suit over her hips before lifting her to remove it the rest of the way. Her thong winked at him from between the round globes of her derrière, flimsy and audacious at the same time, like something a French harlot might wear in a bygone era. The image aroused him and gave even greater form to the beast inside him, lending it claws with which to break its way out.

And then he was scraping his teeth along the same trail his caressing palms had taken, tasting her from behind while she cried out his name, the sound an entreaty and a plea at the same time. He happily obliged until she trembled, her body shaking as it dove into bliss.

It wasn't enough to taste her anymore. He needed to possess her. To break her into a thousand pieces and make each and every one of them irrefutably his.

Pulling away from her, he realized he was still fully clothed, but rather than delay to remedy the fact he simply unbuckled his belt and slipped himself free of his trousers. He was straining and hard and ready.

He made quick work of positioning himself behind her before sliding in, thick and heavy meeting wet and tight, against the backdrop of her helpless moans.

He managed to make three long, slow strokes before the beast demanded more. More speed. More pressure. More intensity.

The fire burning inside him was stoked to an explosive level as Mina's cries echoed in the rounded architecture of her bedroom. His hips became pistons, moving in and out of her, helpless to do anything but return over and over again.

Her body was slick with sweat and he sensed her peaking. But he wouldn't allow her release until she felt like him: weak-willed, insatiable, and selfish. Hammering deep inside her, their bodies in a single rhythm, he refused to take them both over the edge until he knew he wasn't alone and never would be—not in this.

And when she gasped, crying, "Please, Zayn!" and her inner muscles desperately clenched around him, he knew it was true and they detonated.

Hours later, well past midnight, she lay deeply asleep, un-haunted by the ghosts of her father and the wreckage of the evening. He envied her. He was not faring so well on that front, and lying in her bed, listening to the quiet sounds and murmurs of her sleep, wasn't going to make it any better.

What he really needed was a drink. A drink would be the answer to the gnawing craving inside him that seemed to return the instant it was satisfied. He refused to let it be anything else. It was absolutely not the woman who stole his breath, and his attention, and his focus by her simple existence.

Sliding out of her bed, he ignored the tight squeeze the motion brought to his chest. There was no point lying beside her, drawing her into his arms, trusting they would sort everything out in the morning. That was foolish and, worse, neglectful.

He had a job to do.

And he would do it with a drink.

He would call for one as soon as he was out of her rooms. It would be waiting for him on his desk—sharp, no ice, and doubtless strong, just the way he liked it—when he got to his office.

"Where are you going?"

He spun around. She lay on her side, sheets drawn up to cover her breasts. Her head was on the pillow and her stare was wide open.

The image of her like that—relaxed, trusting—clawed at his throat like a choking bramble.

"Go back to sleep." His words were stilted and brittle, tin men in the face of the raw honesty she offered.

"You're leaving."

She didn't say it as a question, and for some reason that rankled him more.

"I have work to do."

"At this hour?"

"At all hours. A king is never off duty," he snapped.

"Typically, it requires a national emergency to force the King into working in the wee hours. Unless I missed an emergency, I can't imagine what is calling you."

This time when he snapped, it wasn't just his voice. "Tonight was an emergency, Mina. An enormous disaster. What's 'calling me' is the need to get my head out of whatever *this* is—" he gestured toward her and the bed "—and back into my work. Unlike you, Mina, people depend on my ability to do my job well."

She winced, her fists tightening on the sheets, but didn't break eye contact with him. "There's no reason to be nasty."

But she was wrong. There was every reason. He had made a fool of himself, and therefore a fool of Cyrano. And all over her.

"There is every reason to be nasty. I swore to myself I would not make the same mistakes my father made—that I would never put my own feelings before the health and safety of my country."

"I don't see how tonight—" she began.

But he cut her off. "Of course you don't see. You may be brilliant, Mina, but don't kid yourself. You're no political mind. Tonight was a travesty, and it was all because I couldn't keep my head together."

"What do you mean?" she asked.

Her obvious desire to soothe him only added fuel to the fire.

"You, Mina. I'm talking about *you*. When you're around I lose control, and that's something a king can't afford. I'm not willing to put the kingdom at risk because I'm in love with you, Mina."

The words shot out—an accusation even more than a confession.

They hung in the air between them, heavy, throbbing, raw.

She searched his face, capturing his gaze with her green and golden stare before asking. "You're in love with me?"

The air whooshed out of him silently, as if he'd been punched in the gut. Still the words hung suspended in air, almost visible, seeming so tangible. She waited for him to answer, and there was grace rooted in her quiet steel. She waited for the truth.

He nodded.

When he did not offer more, she frowned. Then she nodded too, the movement a communication with herself rather than a response to his gesture. It was sinking in—what he was saying to her.

Finally, after the silence had stretched between them and gone past comfortable, she asked, "And you think that's a threat to national security? So you're leaving me, in secret, in the middle of the night?"

Looking deep into the clear sage of her eyes, noting their growing sheen, he pinched off the voice inside him that said he could forge a new path—a stronger path—with the woman he loved at his side, and instead he answered her, "Yes."

He saw his words strike her, saw the gutted agony flash across her gaze and even felt it in himself. He wrenched at it, writhing even as he stood motionless, watching her collapse inside herself. And, unable to bear witness to the havoc he was wreaking, he turned on his heel and walked out.

He walked through the twisting corridors all the way to his office, where he locked himself in on the pretense that he needed to begin developing damage control strategies with Farden.

Six drinks later he'd spent no time thinking about Farden. Alone in his office, and drunker than he typically allowed himself to get, the reins on his mind turned invariably to Mina. Always Mina.

The sharp, raw edges of that hole inside him offered clarity at least. He needed to get away from her. He couldn't go to the summer palace. Not now. Not after the time they'd spent there. Her memory would be everywhere. It would be like surrounding himself with potent traces of the woman he couldn't shake off.

He needed to get away from her—and sooner rather than later. Only time and distance would be sufficient to suffocate the thing that had taken root inside him.

He arrived in Paris through a private airport just before three a.m. A driver took him from there to the apartment his family kept on the Champs-élysées, and he watched the dark streets of the City of Lights pass by through his window. The cobblestoned streets and sidewalks were deserted this deep into the night, each *arrondissement* at quiet rest in preparation for another day of making up the city of Paris.

Stepping out of the car, he looked up to take in the French apartment. It was the first time he had been here in at least three years, and when he tried to name the sensation drawing his heart down into his gut the word that came to mind was *regret*.

That was absurd, however. Regret was a luxury a king could not afford. He did not regret. He merely wished he had brought Mina along, wondering how she would have received the opulent

Parisian apartment, which was classic, traditional, and all things French.

Imagining her wonder brought a smile to lips as he rode the elegant antique elevator to the apartment. But a scowl replaced his smile just as the elevator doors opened, revealing the long hallway that led to the royal apartment. Striding down the hallway, he gave the door guards each a stormy nod before they opened the doors for him.

Inside, he headed straight for the study—and the liquor cabinet. Moving with all the deliberateness and yet none of the care he usually took, he selected a highball glass and rummaged through the assortment of crystal decanters available, all filled with glowing liquids in colors ranging from jewel-toned deep ambers to painfully clear.

He poured his drink rakishly and replaced the decanter with a clatter, uncaring of his lack of grace. There was no audience here. Unlike the kiss at the ball, and the brawl before dinner, there was no one here to bear witness to his absolute lack of decorum.

"Zayn!"

He didn't turn around at once. He simply closed his eyes with a sigh, brought one hand to rub the bridge of his nose and set the glass down with the other. Then he turned around.

A woman stood in the doorway, one hand on

her hip, the other pointing toward him, her silhouette backlit by the bright living area behind her.

"Mother."

The light flicked on. His mother no longer stood in the doorway but walked toward him, her silk pajamas flowing with her movements as she put the safety catch on the small pistol she held as she walked.

"This is unexpected," she said.

Though it was four in the morning, she showed no sign of tiredness, no hint apart from her clothing that he'd woken her from sleep. As always, she was perfect. Elegance personified. It wasn't on purpose. In fact, his memories of childhood were full of her eager efforts to disrupt her own natural grace—so at odds with the fire of her personality—to no avail. With her long white-blond hair, delicate bone structure, and wide violet stare, the blue of her blood had shown through even the thickest mud. And all of it had aged well.

"I didn't know you were in residence," he replied—because it was true. He had not thought to check her whereabouts in his eagerness to escape Mina.

"I only just arrived," she said.

Silence stretched between them, two sets of matching eyes meeting each other across the gulf of the room.

Finally, she said, "You married."

And as if the soft, sad words were the spark the dry tinder of his temper had been waiting for, and because tonight was apparently the night he lost all control, the words, "Did you know?" were ripped out of him, raw and acidic because they made him vulnerable.

Startled confusion replaced the look of hurt in her eyes and she demanded, in a stronger voice, "What in the world are you talking about?"

"Did you know about the betrothal?" he barked, willing to make his own demands.

"Young man. You may be the King of Cyrano, but I am your mother and you will speak to me with respect."

"Like you and father respected me? What about my right to choose?"

"Don't be so dramatic, Zayn. There are worse things than finding yourself married to a beautiful, accomplished woman."

"How do you know she's any of those things?" he asked.

The hurt had returned to her voice when she responded. "I've been following the news."

His attempt at censure might not have found their mark, but hers did. "We were married in private by the Archbishop. Not what you would call a wedding."

"A mother still wants to witness such an event."

"There was no event. I told you. Just the two of us and the Archbishop."

His mother frowned. "Surely her parents were there?"

Zayn shook his head, a feeling of defensive shame growing in his gut at his mother's expression. "No," he said.

"Why not?" she asked, and a dangerous and growing note of suspicion entered her voice with each successive question.

"There wasn't time."

"There wasn't time to invite her parents to her wedding?"

Again, Zayn shook his head. "My men had trouble locating her. She does not go by the name used on the betrothal document. I did not want to risk losing track of her once we found her."

"You make her sound like some kind of criminal."

Zayn flinched, thinking back to his use of the national riot team to collect her.

"I had no idea *who* she was."

Finally, he was able to turn some of the censure around. And this time it was his mother who flinched.

Lifting her hands, palms up, she offered, "We always thought you'd get out of it."

For a moment he just stared at her incredulously. "I had the best lawyers in the country look over the contract. It's unbreakable."

She nodded. "Of course. You were the only one who could have broken it. Or her, I suppose…"

A fluttering sensation entered Zayn's chest at his mother's words. He didn't recognize it as panic because he had never experienced it before. He took a seat on the studded leather sofa. Did his mother know some way that Mina might nullify the marriage? If she was free to walk away, would she?

Palms going clammy, Zayn asked cautiously, "Is there some way we could render the marriage void?"

Mistaking the thread of fear that wove through his words for desperation, his mother took a seat beside him, her eyes widened in alarm. "Oh, no, darling. I'm so sorry. It's far too late now. We just never in a million years thought it would take you so long to find love…"

Her voice trailed off, and the slick, oily panic that had coated Zayn's throat at her words began to dissolve.

The marriage stood.

"What do you mean?" he asked.

His mother's alarm warped into guilt before his very eyes, and for the first time in his life he had the experience of seeing his mother ashamed. "We just never thought it would come to this."

He raised an eyebrow "Somehow I find that hard to believe. Father entered into an agreement that would require constitutional amendment."

"That's absolutely absurd. Absolutely." Like a tempest, his mother blew through emotions like mere changes of clothes. Now indignation ruled. "You're the King—you can't marry a cabbage farmer's daughter!" she exclaimed.

The sentiment was the last thing he'd expected from his mother, who had spent her time as Queen championing the rights of the poor, and Zayn found himself bristling in Mina's defense.

"Mina is far more than just a cabbage farmer's daughter, Mother—far more. And, thanks to Dad, we are already married."

The fact that he'd used the cold, commanding tone he reserved for speaking from the throne on his mother startled them both.

She opened her mouth to speak, but closed it again.

Uncomfortable with this discord with his mother, but unwilling to back down in his protection of Mina, he surprised himself by adding, "Besides, you don't even know that her father grew cabbage."

His mother took her seat once more, her eyes growing shrewd. "Of course I know her father grew cabbage. I know everything about the man."

It was Zayn's turn to be confused. "What do you mean?"

"I was pregnant with you—just weeks away from my due date—when I developed anemia. My hemoglobin levels dropped below three and my doctors insisted I needed a blood transfusion. Obviously they looked to Seraphina first, but I have a rare blood type and she wasn't a match. They searched the national donor database, invoked royal privilege to search all private medical records, and even reached out to distant cousins amongst Europe's royal families, but still could not find a match. Then your father had them search an old military database—and would you believe it? A match with a former sergeant. Ajit Aldaba—the one person on the entire island who could save my life."

Zayn's mouth dropped open, hanging wide in the same fish expression he'd accused Mina of having.

Clearly exhausted by the telling, his mother continued, "Your father was out of his mind with worry. My pregnancy had been rocky from the beginning, and we wanted you more than anything in the world. By then we knew I would not likely be able to sustain another pregnancy, so even though there was a risk we approached Sergeant Aldaba."

Zayn's voice rasped out, a dagger in the darkness. "And he said yes, on the condition you gave away your only son in a betrothal?"

His mother's eyes widened, catching enough light in the dim room to shine a clear amethyst. "Oh, no. No. Nothing like that." Her eyes went a bit misty before she continued. "No. He said yes without hesitation... He was about to have a daughter—she was due just after you—and he said he hoped anyone would do the same for his wife. And, of course, he was a soldier through and through, always ready to answer the call '*for the good of Cyrano.*'" She smiled at the memory.

The echo of the same words he'd heard in Mina's voice pierced Zayn's heart like a poisoned dart. Then his mother shook her head, as if the images were a fog.

"No. It was your father who took it further," she continued.

"What?"

"That man." She crossed her arms in front of her chest, irritated still, even thirty-six years later. "He offered the man anything under the sun— insisted he chose a gift when he initially refused. He even had the gall to remind him to think of his growing family. It was that that did it, really."

"Did what?"

"Gave him the idea to ask for your hand in marriage."

Zayn would have laughed at her turn of phrase

if farcical history had not been the stuff of his destiny.

"After your father had all but commanded him to ask for something, and then reminded him of his coming daughter, he threw out the idea of marriage. I think he was joking, really, but once the words were out things snowballed."

"What do you mean, 'things snowballed'?" Zayn's didn't bother to hide his irritation when he spoke.

"I was out of it after the transfusion. Ajit was out of it too. Your father was out of his mind with relief that both you and I had made it through the procedure alive. He needed a grand gesture to show his gratitude. One thing led to another and you were betrothed."

"You make it sound like a one-night stand," he observed drily.

The Queen snorted, continuing, "Your father regretted it before we even left the hospital. So much so that he went back to Ajit—and you know how much pride he had."

As usual, his mother was siding with his father, but her statement, could not go unremarked upon. "I should think so. He was a great proponent for choice and true love, after all."

His mother lifted her eyebrow. "You're emoting rather loudly, dear."

He scoffed. "I'd say I have the right."

"This side of you is all your father."

He ignored that. "You were saying…? He felt bad?"

"He swallowesd his pride and went back to Ajit to amend the agreement. They added a clause. *If neither child should find love before they turn thirty-five, the two shall be joined…* It was a small addition, but we all felt it would do the job."

Zayn didn't try to hide his exasperation. "This is all absolutely absurd, you do realize? You were real monarchs, you know—not fairy tale characters."

She chuckled. "I was on a lot of drugs at the time. And your father… He would have done anything for us."

The look on her face said she was momentarily lost, caught up in the memory of the man she'd loved more than any other soul save the son who stood before her. She came back, though.

"Besides, thirty-five seemed like plenty of time—eons away at the time. Of course, it all flew by faster than we could ever have realized…"

Watching his mother, knowing he was about to lose her to the pull of sorrow, as he had so many times since his father had died, he made his voice bitter when he said, "I should have known."

"Should have known what?" she asked, reluctantly drawn back from the pull of his father's memory.

"I should have known that his unhealthy attachments were at the root of all this."

An edge came to her voice as she lifted her eyebrow to say, "Excuse me?"

"I should have expected this entire fiasco had its roots in Dad's obsessive love."

His mother gasped. "Zayn Darius d'Argonia. How dare you speak of your father like that?"

"My father put love before his duty to the nation time and time again. When he decided to let the prime minister handle public hearings two days a week so the two of you could spend quality time together. When he postponed the national exposition because your due date approached… And this—sacrificing my future, not to mention the fate of the nation, just to say thank you." Disgust dripped from his words.

There was a moment of silence before his mother finally replied, her voice dry as desert sand. "Saving one's wife and child requires something a little stronger than a thank-you, Zayn. But, since you appear inclined toward hyperbolic oversimplification at the moment, I won't be the one to argue with you."

Just as she had always been able to, his mother lanced the boil of his self-righteous anger, revealing his asinine behavior in the process.

He brought his thumb and forefinger up to pinch the bridge of his nose. "I'm sorry."

His mother closed the distance between them and hugged him. "I accept your apology. I am sorry, too. I had no idea you felt that way."

"It doesn't matter."

She shook her head. "No. It's important. Your father would be the first to acknowledge that he put his loved ones before everything, but that's what made him such a great king. He *loved*, Zayn. He loved so fiercely he was willing to sacrifice everything, over and over. But never you."

Zayn reeled. So many pieces of his family puzzle were rearranging themselves in a single instant that the very foundation of his identity shook.

"We never told you before because—well, because it's so complicated. There was so much we didn't tell you. But the betrothal, at least, we thought would never become an issue. We were so sure you would find love long before the terms were up. As the date got closer we decided to tell you when you turned thirty-four. But then the assassination…"

So much had happened in the six months immediately following his father's death—his coronation, the discovery of his uncle's plot, his uncle's death, his mother's departure. His memories of the time were hazy and dark, but one thing was becoming clear.

"Father was right."

Frowning, his mother asked, "About what, dear?"

Instead of explaining how this new information had shed light on the shadows of his narrative, chasing away the monsters he'd feared lived in their depths, he said, "I have to go back to Cyrano," and kissed his mother's cheek.

His mother started. "Right now? But you've only just got here. And it's so late."

But he was already making his way to the door.

CHAPTER ELEVEN

THERE HAD BEEN no word from the King.

The morning after he'd left Mina had waited in her office, sure he would come to make amends for the way they had parted.

He had not.

So she had walked purposefully to the staff office and found the King's major domo and his assistant deep in discussion with the chef when she arrived. Each of them had looked up and straightened when they'd seen who stood before them.

"Get me the King on the phone."

For the first time since toddlerhood, Mina hadn't said *please*. He owed her an explanation and she wasn't going to beg or wait for it.

All three staff members had immediately bowed, working in unison to coordinate locating a phone, dialing, and placing it into her palm.

And as the cold device had touched her skin, it had brought with it the realization that she was

the Queen of Cyrano, with all her rights and priv-
ileges.

It hadn't been the Archbishop marrying her in
the chapel, or wearing a solid gold mask to her
debut ball, or visiting the private summer palace,
or playing international stratagems that had made
it sink in. It had been the fact that she could walk
into a room and demand to speak with the King
and have it be done.

The line had rung. And rung. And rung. After
the fourth ring, his voicemail had picked up, and
his voice had been a slick lick of fire in her core,
despite all her frustration.

Mina had not left a voicemail. Neither had
she let her mouth fall open in outrage, and nor
had she made any noise to indicate how infuri-
ated she was. Instead, she had sucked in a breath
through flared nostrils, held out the phone to one
of the three staff members, who had taken it with
a slight tremors in his hand, and then she had
turned and left the room.

For dinner that night she had ordered every single one of her favorite foods, called up a priceless
bottle of wine, and dined alone while watching
period costume dramas, crying only at the appropriate plot points.

And now, this morning, still with no sign of
the King, she had returned to carrying out her
duties, projecting an image of a warm and dot-

ing wife when in reality she was hurt and angry enough that she might have taken her own unannounced vacation.

But, no, that wasn't her. Regardless of how anyone else around her behaved, she would always live up to her own standards.

She had kept her word, enacting every duty required of her as outlined in her schedule, which had included two video calls with heads of state and responding to a number of letters and requests.

This evening, though, there was a shared event on their calendar. On national television.

A public reunion after his abandoning her was perhaps poor planning on his part, but after her failed attempt at reaching out to him she hadn't been willing to try again. She had some pride.

And she had something else, too. It was strange and powerful and new, but she recognized the feeling that coursed through her for what it was: rage.

Shaking her head to clear it of thoughts of him, Mina turned to d'Tierrza. "Roz and her team aren't due for another hour," she said.

D'Tierrza smiled. "So you expect them any minute?"

"Exactly. Though for the life of me I don't know why she seems to delight in catching me off guard so much. You'd think she'd want me cooperative."

"She wants you too confused to say no to her."

"What do you mean by that?" Mina asked—just as Roz and her team burst into the suite.

Mina sighed, but only because she knew she would never get her answer now, rather than over the frenzy that was about to begin. She welcomed that. It was just enough of a distraction—and the only form of armor she had—to keep her mind off the fact that she would be in the same room with Zayn again in a matter of hours.

Tonight, though, she dressed for herself—not for her husband, not for her role as Queen, not for academia, and not for her father. Just for her.

Tonight, she and the King would appear together on the *Jasper Caspian Show*—the most popular late-night show in all of Cyrano—and tonight, and for evermore, she would be herself.

She caught the makeup artist's eye. "Tonight, I want to be as flawless as you."

Sabine laughed, the faintest pink showing on her cheeks as the only sign that she had taken the Queen's words in. "Impossible," she said dismissively—only to ruin the effect with a wink and the words, "But I'll get you damn close."

Mina turned to her wardrobe next. "This will be my biggest audience yet. I want to show the world the everyday Queen Amina, while also looking breathtaking. And I want comfortable shoes. Can you make that happen?"

Catriona snorted and rolled her eyes. "Isn't that exactly what I do every time?"

Mina laughed, shaking her head as she turned to her hairdresser. "Down and free tonight," she said. "I'm tired of tying myself in knots and shrinking myself to fit. Big hair—don't care."

Byron smiled warmly, showing full teeth. "Great minds, Your Majesty." Then he inclined his head toward her, adding a small flourish with a twirl of his comb.

Finally, she came to Roz and her assistant. "How did I do?"

Roz snorted, the sound dry for all that it was nasal. "You managed to get your point across. Passable. An autumnal seventies theme will tie everything together. You're going to charm the nation tonight."

Coming from Roz, that last declaration might as well have been a tearful embrace.

Mina raised an eyebrow. "And here I was, thinking I'd done that with the Queen's Ball."

"Pish. You stunned them then. Absolutely stopped them in their tracks with just an image. Tonight, they'll see you alive, moving, speaking, breathing—your darling, refreshing, self on full display."

Mina winked at Chloe, Roz's assistant, before

saying, "Be careful, Roz. All that praise might go to my head."

Roz's voice crackled as it rolled out as casually and slowly as sagebrush. "Keep in mind that 'refreshing' can get old."

D'Tierrza smothered a laugh from wherever it was she had faded into the background and Mina pretended to be offended when, really, she was nearly as content as she had ever been.

In all her years of research, Dr. Amina Aldaba would never have predicted that here she would stand, in a palace, surrounded not by colleagues, but by true, real friends. An unexpected rag-tag bunch they might be, but they were real.

Make-up came first. Once again, Sabine used colorful powders to draw out the gold and green flecks in Mina's eyes, but this time, rather than smoky, the palette the woman chose held tones which could only be described as down-to-earth—rich, deep browns, buttery tans, and shimmering cream.

Wardrobe came next, and Mina pulled on the soft, snug-fitted cashmere sweater they had picked out for her. The sweater was the color of ripe pomegranates and had a simple and elegant wide crew neck. It was paired with a pleated midi-length A-line skirt in the same color, and a thin tan leather belt that cinched her at the waist. The espadrilles that went with it were gorgeously comfortable, as well as flattering, and immediately became Mina's favorite royal footwear.

Her hairstylist left her hair down, using his comb to add mountains of volume and his curling rod to define and touch up individual curls here and there. The highlights he had given her before combined with the artfully tousled curls to make her look simultaneously natural, sexy, and straightforward all at once. She couldn't have asked for better.

When she looked in the mirror, she finally saw herself. Queen Mina. Not boxed-up Dr. Aldaba, and not the bursting star of Queen Amina. Just simple, lovely, honest, and kind Queen Mina. A common woman of the highest quality, showcased as much by the open expression on her face as by the top-tier fabrics she wore.

Her face was, if not flawless, near perfection. Light and breathable, her makeup looked like it was barely there, even as it highlighted and sculpted her features, emphasizing her eyes and lips in a way that made her blush at her reflection.

Her eyes reflected not just her recently revealed beauty—beauty that even she could appreciate now—but also the intelligence that she had worked so hard for.

She wasn't merely a pretty distraction for her nation. She wasn't merely a brilliant scientist—or even just a gifted linguist and scholar. She was a multifaceted queen, not only fit, but ideally suited to the job.

She had even almost earned the love of her King. She'd known it in the desperate way he'd held her the night before he'd left.

And now, like the straw and smoke they were, her hollow attempts at mental bolstering faltered and dispersed, and she was left standing in front of a mirror, about to join Zayn for an interview, to sit beside him under the public's scrutinizing gaze, knowing that she had offered him everything she had and he had refused it.

But she didn't let any of that show on her face. The people around her had worked too hard to make her look pretty for her to let them down with a frown.

Nothing got past hawk-eyed Roz, though. Catching Mina's eye in the mirror, the woman said, in an overloud voice, "Since it's late-night, we wanted to go with something earthy and sensual while remaining well within the bounds of propriety. With your perfect height and coloring that obviously meant updated nineteen-seventies casual glamour."

Mina's smile finally reached her eyes. "Obviously."

"If anyone asks you who you're wearing, tell them you don't know. It'll be nonchalant and more natural for you, since you'll never remember if I tell you. We sent a press release—they can find the answer there."

"Should I be expecting that kind of question?"

Roz snorted. "Of course. This is television. All they really care about is fashion and sex."

Mina blushed, the heat deepening the brown of her cheeks and setting off her makeup highlights charmingly. The aesthetician was really a magician.

"Let's hope not." She laughed through it. "I'm better versed in biochemistry."

Roz waved her away. "Yes. Well, one can't help one's shortcomings…"

D'Tierrza's laughter bounced around the room, and the sound of it eased some of the squeeze around Mina's heart.

She squared her shoulders and turned to her two guards. "Shall we go?"

Moustafa nodded, a faint smile softening the seriousness with which she did everything. D'Tierrza grinned like a fox.

Roz draped a sleeveless cape over her shoulders, and handed her a small leather clutch that matched her belt.

Mina turned to her team. "Thank you, as always. Your magic amazes me." To Roz, she said, "You're a queen-maker."

Roz rolled her eyes. "Of course I am. Now, go. And expect miracles."

Mina opened her mouth to ask a follow-up question, but d'Tierrza was already drawing her away.

Stepping into the barrage of flashing lights, microphones and cameras was by far the most challenging thing Mina had done yet as Queen. There had been a red carpet and press at the Queen's Ball, but nothing compared to the walk from her car to what was supposed to be the private entrance for guests on the *Jasper Caspian Show*.

Perhaps it was the combination of royalty and television, but it was all Mina could do to keep a smile plastered on her face and answer the odd question.

When someone shouted, "Who are you wearing?" she turned the plastered-on smile in their direction.

"I have no idea," she said. Just like Roz had told her to.

"What's your favorite sex position?"

She was saved from acknowledging that question by reaching the end of the gauntlet.

Once inside the studio, she closed her eyes, drawing in a long, slow, deep breath before opening them and looking around.

Everything was painted black and, industrial as a result of form and function rather than design. Soundproofed walls separated the set and studio audience from what went on backsta which mostly appeared to be men walking around with clipboards wearing dark, loose-fitting clothing and headsets.

One such man, slender, pale, and young, with shaggy brown hair and a pair of dusty black cargo pants, met Mina and her guards at the door.

"Right this way, Your Majesty," he said as he ushered her toward a door set apart from most of the backstage traffic.

She grimaced at his form of address, but appreciated the rescue. Inside, the room was a shock of cozy warm-toned beige and tan, with a coffee table set with a lovely bouquet of flowers and refreshments, and an arrangement of plush furniture.

"We've prepared the green room according to your secretary's instructions, but don't hesitate to let us know if there is anything you need."

Unaware that she'd even given instructions in the first place, Mina merely nodded with the words, "Thank you."

The King had not arrived by the time the stage manager came to escort her, ready for her cue, so she walked onstage alone.

The lights on the stage were too bright for her to make out the live audience, for which she was grateful. She didn't need to see the faces of the people she was worried about making a fool of herself in front of, on top of everything else.

Though she couldn't make them out in detail, she could tell that they, like Jasper Caspian, at his famous desk, came to their feet as she entered the stage. The stage band played the last chords of the national anthem as she took the seat nearest to Jasper's desk, knees together, legs crossed at the ankles, as Roz had instructed.

Angled toward him for their conversation, she got her first view of Jasper Caspian, up close and personal. The first thing that struck her was how large his head was. Not only was it slightly over-sized for his frame, it was particularly round. Coupled with his large eyes, it made him look faintly like a cartoon come to life.

Knowing it contributed to his visual interest and appeal, the biologist in her was fascinated.

His hair was white-blond and…*swoopy*. That was the only word for it. Thick, silky, and swoopy. His eyes and eyebrows were deep brown, a star-tling contrast to the rest of his fair coloring, and the combination was likely what he owed his rise to stardom to.

He studied her in return, his expression cun-ning as he took in every detail. And as the wild cheering of the audience settled, Jasper's smile grew.

When they'd finally sat down in their seats and quietened, he said, "I'd say let's give the Queen of Cyrano a warm welcome, but any warmer than that and we'd be breaking our fire codes!"

The audience laughed at his joke, but sedately, as he'd clearly wanted. Obviously he was an expert at managing the energy of a large group of people.

Mina was impressed.

"So, Queen Mina—that's what they told me to call her, folks, we're not being fresh—you're finally here. The mysterious, multitalented woman who captured our King's...heart."

The man imbued his pause with the energy of salacious wink and the audience ate it up.

Mina couldn't help the smile that spread across her own face, despite recognizing in him each and every class clown she'd ever had the challenge of teaching. It made her happy to think of any one of them finding their place in the world, as Jasper so clearly had.

"We're all dying to know...well, *everything*. Start with that."

Mina waited for the laughter to die down before saying, "Well, I suppose I should start where it all began."

Jasper leaned in. "Yes. Do."

Mina laughed, unable to fight her growing ease in his presence. She moistened her lips, smiled wide, and said, "It begins with Cyrano, of course. In fact, I was born and raised right here in the capital. A dyed-in-the-wool, tried-and-true, homegrown Cyranese capital rat."

Jasper's eyes flashed his admiration even as he smiled. "That's right...that's right," he said. "They're calling you 'the commoner who caught a king.' You are the very first commoner to marry into the royal family in Cyranese history. Did you know that?"

Mina did not know that—had not, in fact, even ever thought of it. But, rather than miss a beat, she simply admitted it, saying, "No. I had no idea. I must admit for most of my life I've been focused on being appointed to the King's council."

Jasper's smile widened. "Indeed, you are a queen of firsts. But, of course, what we all really want to hear about is how you snared the most eligible bachelor in the kingdom."

Mina opened her mouth to reply, only to be drowned out by the collective gasp of the audience and Jasper at her side.

All the attention in the room was focused on the man walking on stage to join her. And then the audience was on their feet once again.

Without needing to turn, she knew it was Zayn. But when she did turn, he looked different.

First and foremost, he had the beginnings of a beard, the dark stubble lending the hard planes of his face a sense of warmth and wisdom. His hair was styled neatly, but more naturally. And that was not the most dramatic change.

For the first time since his father's death, the King wore a color other than black.

Admittedly, the very deep navy of his trim suit was not a far jump from his usual palette, but in someone as closely scrutinized as the King, the difference might as well have been a shout. Like a monarch of old, he had come out of mourning.

In his lapel pocket was a burst of flowers, their colors a complement to her own attire.

Breathless, she watched him cross the stage, his long legs eating up the short distance quickly.

His scent enveloped her, an erotic caress in the room full of people, as he reached around her to shake Jasper's hand in greeting. It wasn't the King's first appearance on the show.

He sat on the other side of Mina, his body language relaxed and open, for all the world to examine. She wished she could project that kind of ease when she didn't feel it.

"Welcome, Your Majesty. It's lovely to have you back on the show—even if you are late."

Zayn smiled at the mock censure in the other man's tone, and there was a great sense of contentment in his expression. "I apologize for that. Traffic in this city is just out of control. Someone should do something about that…"

The audience laughed, just as Zayn had intended, and Mina enjoyed the thrill of pride that came with recognizing that he was more than a match for Jasper.

And he was hers.

At least on paper.

She was getting used to the stabbing sensation in her chest whenever her mind lingered on him too long.

"Well, before you distracted all of us with your arrival, our lovely Queen Mina here was going to reveal to us all how she captured your heart."

Zayn caught her eyes then. The violet of his gaze was warm and welcoming, with no hint of the resistance she knew he was committed to.

And yet despite that, even in front of an audience, she was still arrested by the locking of their gazes, frozen and lost at the same time.

He would forever be the most beautiful man she had encountered in her life.

His lips curled up at the edges and she felt the movement deep in the wet heat of her core.

"Oh, was she, now?" he said, drawing out the words with a suggestiveness that had her blushing. "I'd love to hear that."

Jasper grinned, sensing the kind of show content that spiked ratings lurking in the heightened awareness thrumming between them, and Mina swallowed.

"Then again," Zayn said, drawing the focus to

himself effortlessly, "you could just get the information from the source."

Jasper turned to the audience. "What do you think audience? His or hers?"

Mina's stomach dropped, and in that instant she realized she didn't know which would be worse: hearing his answer, or having to fabricate her own.

The audience, it seemed, was most concerned with accuracy, choosing to go with testimony from the primary source, and Mina braced her heart—as much as it was possible to brace the kind of organ that attached itself to another person regardless of whether or not he reciprocated that attachment or not.

Zayn turned a wide smile toward the audience, ready to tell some canned lie, no doubt. "Now. You were asking how to win a king's heart?"

Jasper pointed to the King and said, "This guy!" before shrugging and adding the words, "Close enough."

The audience laughed, but quietened quickly. They wanted to hear what he said.

Mina's stomach turned.

He slipped his hand around hers and squeezed, before beginning. "It helps to be the most brilliant scientist in the country. That's a strong first step to getting caught by a king."

Rather than cringe, Mina found herself fighting the urge to snort. Getting "caught by a king" was certainly one way to say *getting arrested*. The tight knot in her chest eased just a fraction.

Jasper pretended to take notes on his desk. "Step one: be a rocket scientist."

Zayn laughed along with the audience, the sound unfettered and genuine and, for Mina, completely disorienting.

"Next," he said, "one must naturally be stunningly beautiful."

Jasper nodded mock seriously, "Naturally."

"But I don't mean just ordinary beauty. I mean a beauty that collects everything there is to love about our island nation and puts it into the form of a woman."

An instant of silence greeted Zayn's statement, wherein not even Jasper Caspian could think of something clever to say.

The words sank into all of Mina's soft tissues, anchoring themselves in a way that she knew would make every other compliment pale in comparison for the rest of her life.

The audience recovered first, responding with a loud sigh of longing.

Looking at Mina, Zayn began to speak again. "But that is the mere surface. The kind of sparkling tinsel that catches the eye of every foolish man. In order to truly capture a king, you must first make a habit of squaring your shoulders and facing every challenge head-on."

The tenor of his voice had changed, and despite the fact that he spoke for the all the world to know, in truth it was as if he spoke to his Queen alone.

"You must be cool-headed and controlled when your dreams are crushed. You must be earnest. You must meet every curve ball thrown at you."

Mina's mind was filled with their hasty chapel wedding with the Archbishop, its details becoming even more surreal in memory.

"You must be willing to walk miles when you have just fallen from the sky, finding beauty along the way. You must know how to cook a mean tagine."

Here Jasper broke in with, "A queen that cooks? Now, there's a keeper, folks!"

The audience took the break as an opportunity to let out the collective breath they were holding on a laugh, before leaning closer for more.

Zayn continued, his attention still focused on Mina. "It takes more than a surprising talent to steal a king's heart, of course. You must offer true partnership, a safe haven, and a place to be an ordinary man."

Mina's eyes pricked with the tears, but she would be caught dead before she'd let herself shed them during her first television appearance.

"You must also be willing to stand up against

the opinion of a king. You must be indomitable. You must accept what you cannot change, but demand change when you know you can. Most of all, you must never accept less than you deserve."

Mina swallowed again, the knot in her throat bearing a suspicious similarity in thickness to barely restrained emotion.

Letting Zayn's words rest in the air for a moment, Jasper was less irreverent when he next spoke. "Well, my dears. There you have it. What it took to woo the King. Sounds easy enough— am I right?"

The audience chuckled appreciatively.

Eyes still on Mina, Zayn said, "She certainly makes it look so."

More of that internal knot loosened, even as a part of her grabbed at its strands, trying to keep it together, a tight ball of resentment to block him from digging in any deeper.

Jasper fanned himself. "Folks, it is just as hot sitting here by these two lovebirds as it seems. I admit I didn't expect the change in you, Your Majesty. It seems like it was only a few months ago you were here on this show, a completely different man."

"That's the impact of a good woman."

"I can see why you were so quick to scoop her up into matrimony. Though you denied us all the pomp and fun of a royal wedding!" Jasper's pout was a consummate expert's.

A mischievous glint lit in Zayn's eyes. "You know, Jasper. You're right. I acted quickly when the opportunity presented itself. But you, and certainly my lovely bride, deserve something better than that."

And then he got down on one knee in front of her. Jasper and the audience gasped, and a sheen of tears came to Jasper's eyes that Mina knew had nothing to do with romance and everything to do with ratings.

The audience erupted into applause.

Zayn smiled. "I would marry you every day, Mina. Over and over again."

She wanted to believe him. She did. But they were in front of a live studio audience and he had a scandal he wanted people to forget about. Even though he was asking, he wasn't really.

She had a clear line in this drama and she did her part, nodding, and the cheering went up another few notches before it began to calm down to a reasonable level.

When the moment came, Jasper said, "Well, you saw and heard it on the *Jasper Caspian Show*, folks. We're going to get a royal wedding after all!"

The audience came to their feet in raucous applause and Mina let Zayn clasp her hand, lifting her arm high as they came to their feet before he led her off the stage.

As soon as they entered the green room, however, Mina shook her hand free.

"No," she said.

"What do you mean, 'no?'" he asked.

"I'm not going to marry you again in a big public display in order to distract your people from your recent behavior. Our relationship will not be a tool in your arsenal, and what's more I will not be Queen on your terms. I'm tired of being swept up in the plans and requirements of the men in my life, never being asked what I want. If we're to do this like colleagues, then we keep to business hours and business topics. If we're to be more—" she took a breath before meeting his eyes "—then you owe me an apology."

He stared at her, left her words hanging between them.

She frowned as his silence grew, her eyebrows drawing slowly together and the corners of her mouth tilting down just slightly, her always too revealing eyes wounded. He just watched her as she gave up hope and then squared her shoulders.

She took a breath and said, "I've lived my entire life on other people's terms, Zayn. My father's, academia's, yours…" She used a finger to quickly dash away a falling tear. "I'm done with that now. I will be Queen on my terms. You can contact my secretary to coordinate our activities, but I will not put my heart on the line for a farce."

And she turned her back on him and started toward the door.

"Stop."

The word wasn't a command, but a plea.

She stopped, blowing out a frustrated breath, her heart in her throat.

"You're right. I apologize, Mina."

She turned around, her attention caught.

"I should never have left you like that. I was scared—of what I feel, of how I lose control when it comes to you." He laughed, and the sound was self-recriminatory. "It's not comfortable to know I have it in me to cause a diplomatic incident where you're concerned."

"About that—"

She opened her mouth, ready to tell him that she had secured the relationship with Farden. It had taken a long video-call, in which she had explained what had happened to the Chancellor and bonded with her over their shared love for the same chocolate bar. The call had ended not only with the establishment of a diplomatic relationship, but also a sincere apology from Farden over Werner's conduct.

"It's not important, Mina. Nothing is more important to me than you. Not Cyrano, not being King—not a thing."

Mina's heart thundered but she kept her eyes shuttered. "What changed?"

Facing her, he smiled. "The difference between a boy and man is that a man can admit when he's wrong," he said. "You have made me a better king at every instance, Mina. My loving you is not only no threat to the nation, it will be its savior."

"How do I know you won't disappear again?"

He smiled, likely sensing the weakening of her defenses. "You will have to trust me. But to help…no more separate wings. And we're going to have a real wedding, with both of our mothers in attendance. And this."

He dropped to one knee again, pulling out a small black box.

Opening it to reveal the astounding diamond ring within, he said, "Dr. Amina Elin Aldaba. You alone have shown me what it means to truly love. I can think of no woman better suited to sit at my side as my Queen. Will you marry me?"

Mina nodded through happy tears and a wide grin stretched across her face, her wild curls bouncing with the movement. He slipped the ring on her finger before coming to his feet. Weaving his fingers through the soft springs to cup the back of her head, he pulled her close, and as their lips met she realized that, although she hadn't always known their shape, her dreams had finally come true.

* * * * *

Unable to put
Stolen to Wear His Crown *down?*
Be sure to check out Marcella Bell's
next book in
The Queen's Guard trilogy. Coming soon!